W9-CRO-880

The loop settled over Amy, but also caught Hank

The rope tightened around them with the gentle persuasion of a mare nudging her colt home....

She'd raised her arms when he'd pulled her toward him and her hands rested high on his chest. They rose and fell with his quick breaths, branding him.

The sounds around him drifted away. He lost himself in Amy's green eyes. His hands held the back of her waist, drifted down to her hips. He thought of ripe pears and his blond guitar.

She smelled warm, like the sun, like mango and papaya and coconut. Her skin looked soft enough to lick.

What if he did what he wanted and rested his head on her golden hair, felt the soft glide of it across his cheek? What if he leaned down to press his lips to her eyelids to close them, so she couldn't see all of those handsome cowboys crowding around her? What if he kissed her until she was aware of only plain Hank?

Before he could act on the crazy impulse, she did the oddest thing. She closed her eyes and leaned forward, then smelled him with a delicate sniff.

She opened her eyes and smiled into his. "Soap. Nice."

Dear Reader,

What is a born-and-bred city girl of Irish descent, who grew up in Toronto eating Greek pastries on the Danforth, noshing on grapes from her Italian neighbor's vines and drinking Turkish coffee with her Macedonian friends, doing writing romance novels about cowboys and cowgirls?

They fascinate me! I admire the committed work ethic that compels them to raise cattle under the toughest conditions, to battle summer droughts and winter blizzards to maintain a way of life that has been bred into their bones.

I also love horses, love reading about them and watching them in movies. Sadly, I've never been on one. A hopelessly inept athlete, I never stop trying. Recently I went dogsledding for the first time and came home bruised and euphoric. Rock climbing is next. After that...horseback riding? Maybe it's time to get up close and personal with a real live horse and even, *gulp,* ride one. Wouldn't that be awesome?

I hope you enjoy my debut novel of a rugged cowboy who falls hard for a beautiful city girl.

Mary Sullivan

No Ordinary Cowboy
Mary Sullivan

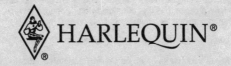

TORONTO • NEW YORK • LONDON
AMSTERDAM • PARIS • SYDNEY • HAMBURG
STOCKHOLM • ATHENS • TOKYO • MILAN • MADRID
PRAGUE • WARSAW • BUDAPEST • AUCKLAND

If you purchased this book without a cover you should be aware
that this book is stolen property. It was reported as "unsold and
destroyed" to the publisher, and neither the author nor the
publisher has received any payment for this "stripped book."

Recycling programs
for this product may
not exist in your area.

ISBN-13: 978-0-373-78315-1

NO ORDINARY COWBOY

Copyright © 2009 by Mary Sullivan.

All rights reserved. Except for use in any review, the reproduction or
utilization of this work in whole or in part in any form by any electronic,
mechanical or other means, now known or hereafter invented, including
xerography, photocopying and recording, or in any information storage
or retrieval system, is forbidden without the written permission of the
publisher, Harlequin Enterprises Limited, 225 Duncan Mill Road,
Don Mills, Ontario, Canada M3B 3K9.

This is a work of fiction. Names, characters, places and incidents are
either the product of the author's imagination or are used fictitiously,
and any resemblance to actual persons, living or dead, business
establishments, events or locales is entirely coincidental.

This edition published by arrangement with Harlequin Books S.A.

® and TM are trademarks of the publisher. Trademarks indicated with
® are registered in the United States Patent and Trademark Office, the
Canadian Trade Marks Office and in other countries.

www.eHarlequin.com

Printed in U.S.A.

ABOUT THE AUTHOR

When Mary Sullivan picked up her first Harlequin Superromance novel, she became hooked on romance. She wanted to write these heartfelt stories of love, family, perseverance and happy endings, about heroes and heroines graced with strength of character and hope. Mary believes that whether we live in the country, the city, or somewhere in between, home is where the heart is, with the people we choose to love.

Don't miss any of our special offers. Write to us at the following address for information on our newest releases.

Harlequin Reader Service
U.S.: 3010 Walden Ave., P.O. Box 1325, Buffalo, NY 14269
Canadian: P.O. Box 609, Fort Erie, Ont. L2A 5X3

To Kelly.
Home is where the heart is.
My heart is with you.

To Maureen, Michele, Molly, Sinead and Teresa.
I couldn't have done this without you.
Thank you.

CHAPTER ONE

"HANK SHELTER, if you're there, pick up!"

Hank ignored his sister's order and strode from the desk to the window, putting distance between him and the telephone.

"Leila," he muttered to his empty office, "I don't feel like tangling with you today. The answering machine can deal with you."

He leaned against the wall beside the open window, his arms crossed, staring across his fields to the distant hills. June in Montana. Was there anything on this earth more beautiful than his ranch?

Correction. Not *his* ranch. *Leila's*. Another of Dad's crazy decisions, to leave the ranch to her. It should have been Hank's. He pounded his fist on the windowsill.

"Hank," Leila continued, "you can't stick your head in the ground like an ostrich and ignore reality."

What reality? Things on the ranch were rolling along just fine.

Leila's sigh over the phone line held a world of frustration.

"Okay, this is the deal. My friend, Amy Graves, is on her way to go over the books. She's an excellent accountant."

An accountant? Hank straightened and uncrossed his arms. What the heck for? He turned to stare at the machine.

He could run this ranch fine on his own, and had been doing so since Dad died.

He'd stopped in at the bank only yesterday and no one had said a word about any problems.

"Wipe the scowl off your face, baby brother," Leila continued, but her tone held a hint of worry under her usual brusqueness. "Cooperate. After the letter I received from the bank this morning, I'm deeply concerned. The situation might have reached the point of no return."

Letter? *What* letter? Point of no return? His heart pounded. Had the bank somehow figured out— They couldn't have. He'd been so careful.

"Someone needs to take control of the ranch's finances before the whole enterprise goes down the toilet."

The toilet? As in losing the ranch? His breakfast threatened a return journey up his throat and he swallowed hard.

Dad's voice echoed through his memory.

"You've screwed up again, boy. Keep it private. We don't need the whole world to know our business."

Shame rushed up from his chest, leaving his cheeks hot enough to melt bullets.

"Hank—" Leila hesitated before saying more. Hank cocked his head. Strange for her to be unsure of anything.

"Amy's fragile these days." Leila's voice held an uncharacteristic softness. "Take care of her."

The solid click of his sister hanging up followed her "goodbye."

Hank clenched his hands and rested them on the windowsill, digging his knuckles into the wood, hoping the pain would eclipse his panic. Even the scents of dust kicked up by horses' hooves and the damp humus of Hannah's garden couldn't calm him now.

Cripes almighty, Leila's sending an accountant to the ranch.

He walked to the desk and shuffled the piles of paper, read the numbers, tried to make sense of Leila's distress.

As far as he could tell, everything was fine. His system was working.

Why would the bank send a letter to Leila, anyway? All the statements came here.

He picked up the phone and dialed the bank, then asked for Donna. She had worked there since before Hank was born. She did Hank's payroll taxes for him, would handle the year-end as she'd done for Dad. If Donna couldn't straighten things out, no one could.

Five minutes later, he hung up. Nope. No problem. The accounts were fine. The bank had no record of a letter being sent to Leila.

Hank heaved a sigh.

Leila was overreacting to something sent to her by mistake. Or whatever. He should call her and tell her what the bank had said. Honest, though, he didn't want to tangle with her today. Once Leila got her mind on something, she was worse than a terrier for not letting go. Next thing, she would come down here to cluck around him like a mother hen, then order him around.

The ranch hands, including Willie, hated taking orders from her. Best just to leave things as they were.

A small voice in the back of his mind warned that Leila was not the kind of woman to run off in a panic for no reason.

Well, he'd get the accountant to relay the message to Leila that all was well here.

He stared at the piles of paper on the desk, on the floor, on every horizontal surface. He might have a great routine that kept things up-to-date and all bills paid, but his filing system was abysmal.

"Keep it private, boy," Dad whispered through his memory again.

"All right," Hank murmured. "I got it the first twelve hundred times."

Even without Dad's harping in his memory, Hank was embarrassed to think of an accountant coming in to see this mess.

He shook his head and returned to the window.

Five of this month's kids, the older ones, saddled horses in the yard for their overnight camping trip.

Wish I could go with them. Next time.

He'd tell the accountant Leila had made a mistake. There was nothing wrong at the bank.

What if she made a fuss, insisted on seeing his books anyway? Damned if he was going to let some city accountant go through his personal stuff, mess up his ranch and his life over nothing. He'd find a way out of this himself—whatever *this* was.

He slammed the window shut and strode to the desk. Dad used to keep a key in the top drawer.

He walked out of the office, turning to lock the door behind him. It hadn't been locked since Dad died. He slipped the key into his pocket.

Down the hallway in the dining room, the younger five of this month's kids, the six- to nine-year-olds, still lingered over breakfast, their chatter mingling with the scents of bacon, eggs and hot chocolate.

Hank peeked in on them. Their baseball caps hung from the backs of their chairs, leaving their delicate scalps exposed.

He clapped his hands. "Who wants to go see the horses?"

They jumped out of their seats and swarmed him, laughing and talking.

He ran a hand over Kyle's soft head, fuzz like freshly seeded grass making a hesitant show.

"Hey, Hank," Jamie yelled, "I can ride a horse good." Some kids did everything full blast, even talking.

Hank grinned.

Quiet Cheryl patted his arm for attention and he picked her up. Her hair resisted regrowth, leaving her skull as bare as a newborn's.

His heart swelled to bursting.

This was what mattered—these children, and keeping the ranch alive for them.

TOO SOON, Amy Graves's twitchy stomach told her she'd arrived at the Sheltering Arms ranch. When she stepped out of her car into the dry heat, a breeze kicked up her bangs and sent them flying around her forehead. It ruffled the feathery branches of a weeping willow that beckoned from the front lawn. A shady refuge.

She took a breath of clean, pure air and tried to calm her nerves. She could do this. She could face this ranch and what it meant to her.

Dust settled on the stretch of dirt road she'd just driven in on from the highway. The driveway bisected golden fields of...what? No clue. *Amber waves of grain.* But what *kind* of grain? One of the things she'd have to find out. What was it and how much profit did they make on it? Or did they feed it to animals, an expense they could claim?

Meadows of green and gold stretched as far as she could see, changing into rolling hills on the horizon.

Above it all, white puffs of cotton candy dotted the huge bowl of brilliant blue that earned Montana the moniker Big Sky.

She sucked in a breath. "Beautiful." She listened to the gentle breeze carrying the distant sounds of children's laughter and her heartbeat slowed, her shoulders relaxed. Calmness crept through her.

A sigh slipped from her lips.

Not fifty yards away, a flock of birds waddled through the grass, older birds leading the flock and young furry chicks following behind. Ducks? Geese? She didn't know the difference.

She was out of her element here. Once a city girl, always a city girl.

The ranch house stood wide, white and placid in the late morning sun. Blue shutters framed windows on the second floor, flower boxes brightened windowsills with yellow pansies. Wicker chairs on the veranda beckoned. *Come and rest a spell, put up your feet, unburden your weary shoulders. Welcome.*

Pretty. She'd expected something rugged, made with logs and adobe or whatever materials people used in the country.

She stepped onto the veranda and heard a cacophony of children's voices approach from the side of the house. A big man with kids dangling from his back, arms and legs rounded the corner of the house. Muscles on top of muscles bulged in his denim shirt and jeans.

Amy smiled. This must be Hank Shelter. Leila said her brother always had children hanging on to him. Amy hadn't known she'd been speaking literally. She counted five children clinging to the man.

Hank leaned down to talk to the two sitting on his feet. "You kids are comin' in for lunch whether you want to or not." His voice, as rough as cowboy boots shuffling on gravel, sent sexy shivers running through Amy.

She rubbed goose bumps from her arms.

The kids answered Hank in varied chirps, "No, Hank, not yet."

"We want one more ride around the house."

"Now kids, we've been around this veranda three times already this mornin' and old Hank ain't gettin' any younger. I gotta wet my whistle and fill my grumblin' belly."

Amy rolled her eyes. Corny. A smile tugged at the corners of her lips.

The man looked up from under the brim of a dusty white cowboy hat. Eyes that shone with the warmth of aged scotch widened when he saw her.

His average-looking face—large nose and strong jaw—would never grace a magazine cover, but a face as bracketed by creases as Hank's was spoke of character.

He snatched the hat from his head, exposing a thick mass of glorious brown hair. One streak of caramel ran across the top of his head from a widow's peak.

Then he smiled and Amy's breath caught. The world was suddenly a brighter place. Good thing he lived under the open Big Sky. He'd eclipse the sun in any other state.

Warmth and sincerity shone from his broad white smile and she felt an answering smile creep across her mouth.

His hazelnut and whiskey eyes sparkled. *My, my.* With only a handful of grins, this man could chase the devil out of a witch's den and have the old crones eating out of his hand.

Crones? Where had that come from? It certainly wasn't a word she ever used in the city. She'd been on the ranch less than five minutes and already she was relaxing into a different lingo.

Amy's hands itched to trim Hank's ragged mustache. *Don't hide a smile so beautiful. Flaunt it.*

Hank Shelter, aren't you a surprise?

One little girl let go of his biceps to wrap her arms around his waist. "I love you, Hank." She gazed up at him with adoring blue eyes.

"Thank you, darlin'," he answered. "A man needs to hear that every so often from a beautiful woman." He rubbed his hand across the child's neck with such tenderness that Amy felt a longing rise in her.

Do that to me.

The young girl giggled and hid her face against his shirt.

When Hank removed his big hand from the back of the child's head, Amy gasped.

From beneath the girl's baseball cap, a bare skull peeked out above a baby-chick neck. A cancer survivor.

Her brief moment of peace shattered. Amy rubbed her chest.

She'd known that the Sheltering Arms ranch took in poor, inner-city kids who were recovering from cancer, and she thought she'd prepared herself for them.

So wrong.

They all wore ball caps with no hair peeking out below. Nothing but more of those delicate bare necks.

The hands Amy wiped on her thighs shook.

The girl turned her face toward Amy. Sallow skin, dark circles under her eyes, thin to the point of pain.

Gulping deep breaths, Amy washed herself with icy aloofness. *Rise above it. Come on, you can do it.*

She turned away and stared hard at the fields, digging deep for strength.

Amy's glance returned to the children against her will, like a tongue probing a sore tooth to see whether pain lingered.

It did.

A boy sitting on Hank's foot pointed to her and asked, "Who is she, Hank?"

HANK'S TONGUE stuck to the roof of his mouth. What was this curvy female, the most beautiful one he'd ever seen, doing on his ranch?

Blond hair. Green eyes. Perfect body. Made a man want to…what? Where were his treasured words when he needed them?

"Exquisite," he whispered. His favorite word. Damn. Hadn't meant to say it out loud.

For a second, he thought she might be mother to one of the children, but he'd met them all in the city a few weeks ago.

"Can I help you, ma'am?" He tried to clear the battery acid out of his voice.

"Are you Hank Shelter?" she asked and her voice washed over him like a Chinook melting February snow. Awareness hummed along his nerve endings.

"Yes, ma'am, I am." Nerves—or the kid clinging to his throat—made him sound rougher than usual.

"I'm Amy Graves, Leila's friend. How do you do, Mr. Shelter?" She extended her right hand toward him.

Leila's friend? "You're the accountant?"

Leila was in her early fifties. Amy didn't look a day over thirty. Didn't that just knock the wind out of him?

He realized his mouth was hanging open and he clamped it shut.

His fingers tingled and his heart pounded. *Slow down,* he warned his treacherous libido.

His body wanted to jump a few fences, but his heart balked at the gates.

He set down the two girls hanging from his right arm, then wrapped his fingers around Amy's hand. It nestled as soft as a calf's ear in his big-galoot palm and started long-forgotten urges. He dropped it like a hot cow pie.

He cleared his throat. "Ma'am, if you'll give me your keys, the kids and I will get your luggage."

The woman nodded.

She's fragile these days.

She looked fit, but he understood what Leila meant about the fragility. Emotional, maybe.

Take care of her.

Uh-uh. No can do. He set his jaw hard enough to hear his teeth grind.

He walked away from her to get her bags, the children following him like a line of baby ducks.

He opened the trunk of her car and pulled out a suitcase and an overnight bag. There was one more bag, supple brown leather with a brass closure. A laptop. *Right,* common sense reminded him. *She's here to work, on the books.*

Too bad, his libido whispered.

Use every trick in the book to get rid of her, his common sense answered. He needed an attraction to the woman who was here to look at his books like he needed a root canal. Not.

He planned to have her hightailing it back to the city by tomorrow morning.

CHAPTER TWO

AMY ENTERED the house and let the screen door butt her back. Her lungs wouldn't expand enough for the air she needed. Maybe coming here hadn't been such a great idea. Sure, she needed to face her fears of illness and dying, but spending time with these children was definitely trial by fire.

She had to do this. Simply *had* to.

She ran a hand over her face, pulling herself under control. The darkness and cinnamon scent of the foyer helped.

Hank entered the house behind her.

"Kids," he said to the children following on his heels, "go wash up. Hannah should have lunch on the table any minute."

They ran down the hall to a room at the far end. Seconds later, someone had the water running.

"That bathroom is across the hall from your bedroom," Hank said. "It'll be your own early mornings and late evenings. The rest of the time, the kids have to use it." He shrugged his apology.

The lemon and soap scent of him drifted by her.

Too nice. Her nerves went on high alert. She was here to test herself with the children. Being attracted—okay, very attracted—to Leila's brother was not in the plan.

Amy followed Hank down the hallway, past a wide staircase leading to the second floor on one side and a closed door on the other. Pastoral landscapes dotted the walls, with not a single abstract in sight. He entered a room at the back of the house, the last one opposite the bathroom the kids were using.

Hank set one of her suitcases onto the floor and the other onto its side on the bed.

"Ma'am, if you don't mind, I'm going to get those kids settled down for lunch. Join us when you finish freshening up."

No. She needed to take exposure to those kids in baby steps.

"I'd like to go straight to the office," she replied. "I'm not hungry."

Her traitorous stomach chose that moment to grumble.

Hank's smile looked smug. "That door leads to the kitchen, where you'll find our housekeeper, Hannah." He pointed behind himself. "The one down the hall is the dining room."

The children ran down the hall away from the bathroom.

"You can't miss it," Hank continued. "Just

follow the sound of those kids. They make enough noise to rouse the dead."

Amy flinched away from that image.

She put on a smile but knew it didn't reach her eyes. The psychic pain she'd been carrying for two years wouldn't quit.

"Dolorous," Hank whispered, then his gaze flew away from hers.

He backed out of the bedroom, bumping into a small table. He caught a vase of lilacs before it fell but not before water sloshed onto his hand. His shoulder bumped into the door frame when he stepped through it. With the vase still in his grasp, he disappeared into the hall.

Well, he couldn't be more different from Leila than chocolate from vanilla. Hard to believe they were related. Hank must be fifteen, sixteen years younger than Leila. Funny. Was Hank a late baby? A midlife surprise for his mother?

No, wait. Leila had mentioned that her mother had died when she was young and her father had remarried. Maybe the second wife was a much younger woman.

Hank had whispered one word on the verandah—*exquisite*. A smile tugged at her lips, the first genuine one she'd felt in ages. She'd pretended not to hear, but it did her soul good that a man found her attractive. Especially these days.

The smile fell from her face.

It doesn't matter, though. Nothing is going to happen here.

She stepped into the hallway and walked toward the dining room. The vase of flowers from her bedroom sat in a puddle on the hallway floor beside the open dining room door.

The suspicion that Hank was a bit of a bumbling gentle giant eased her low mood.

She entered a room swollen with sound. Hank sat at the far end of the table and an older gentleman, who matched Leila's description of the foreman, Willie, sat at the near end. A couple of teenagers sat on one side of the table. Camp counselors? The young children filled in the remaining places, save one. Baseball caps hung from the backs of their chairs. She paused, arrested by the sight of all those bare heads lining the table, too vulnerable in their white roundness, like a nest full of goslings.

She bit her lip.

THERE OUGHT TO BE a law against a woman looking so sweet and beautiful, yet having the potential to be so much trouble. Hank shifted in his seat and watched the accountant walk to the chair beside Willie's, worrying her pretty bottom lip with her teeth.

Hank watched Willie glance up at Amy, his water glass raised to his lips, then do a double take and choke. He slammed the glass back onto the table.

"Willie," Hank said, "meet Amy Graves, Leila's friend. The accountant."

Willie coughed and sputtered into his napkin.

Hank knew how Willie felt. Amy Graves was a shocker. Beautiful. A generation younger than Leila. Smart.

Willie jumped to his feet, pulling Amy's chair out for her. "How d'you do, ma'am? I'm Willie."

Amy shook his hand.

"So, you're stayin' with us the whole summer?" Willie asked after he sat.

"No, only long enough for me to figure out the finances."

Hank's abs tightened.

"Uh-huh. What are you gonna do about the finances?" Willie asked.

Amy's eyes darted to the children. "Well, I'm going to take a look at the books and make some recommendations for Leila."

"Uh-huh? Like what?"

Hank knew that Willie was only making conversation, but this particular discussion didn't belong here, now, in front of the children.

"We can discuss this after lunch," he said and the accountant nodded, the tension around her mouth relaxing. Looked like she didn't want to talk about this in front of the children any more than he did.

They finished Hannah's excellent minestrone

then Amy said "no" to dessert. Watching her weight? Lord, why? He stole a glance at as much of her body as he could see above the table. Her lovely chest rose and fell with her breathing. She wasn't a large woman, nor was she too thin. She was just about right.

Hank finished two servings of Hannah's apple cobbler. Then, while the children lingered over dessert with Willie and the counselors, he asked Amy if she would join him in the living room.

He led her across the hall to the far end of the room and gestured toward one of the two maroon sofas. He sat in an armchair across from her.

"Listen," he started. "There's been a mistake."

She frowned. *Quizzically.* Great word.

"I don't know what kind of letter Leila got from the bank," he continued, "but there isn't a problem here."

"There must be something wrong or the bank wouldn't have sent a letter."

"Did you see it?" Hank asked. "Do you know what it said?"

"No, Leila called me from Seattle. Her boss sent her there this morning to handle a business emergency. She expressed grave concern about the state of the finances here."

"I called the bank this morning," he said, raising his arms and linking his fingers behind his head.

Her gaze dropped to his chest. "What did they say?" she asked.

"That nothing was wrong," he answered. "They didn't send Leila a letter."

Amy's gaze returned to his face. "But I know Leila received a letter."

"I guess you'd better head back to the city and take it up with her."

She looked at his chest again and he realized his shirt was stretched real tight across his pecs. She was staring. Made him feel warm. Self-conscious. He wasn't used to women looking at him like that. She wasn't thinking about money and banks. She was thinking about him and his chest. He lowered his hands to the arms of the chair.

She relaxed against the back of the sofa as if a string stretched tautly from him to her had let go. "I've told her I intend to check things out here, and I will," she said.

"But there's no need," he insisted, his pulse picking up.

"In this situation, as the owner of the ranch, Leila is my boss, and I answer to her." Her voice was quiet, but there was no denying her determination.

There it was, the bald truth he hated so much— that Leila could do whatever she wanted with his ranch, with or without his cooperation. He curled his fingers into his palms.

"What are you looking for?" he asked, unable to hide the belligerence in his tone. He'd been raised better than to treat a guest badly, but his heart rate was shooting through the stratosphere. Leila had been desperate enough to send a stranger here to look at the books. That could only presage bad news.

Presage. He liked that word.

Hank flexed his jaw and narrowed his eyes.

"I'll look for evidence of neglect—" She hesitated, her manner cool now, then said, "Willful misuse of funds."

She couldn't possibly find out, could she?

Mice with sharp claws skittered up Hank's spine, accompanied by foreboding.

Naw, he'd called the bank himself. Things were fine.

"Best-case scenario," she said, "I'll make recommendations on how to maximize your income and minimize your expenses."

Hank's throat burned. His pride ached. It had suffered when Dad had willed the ranch to Leila. Now here it was again, rearing its godforsaken head.

"Worst-case scenario?" Hank asked, his voice even rougher than earlier.

"We can discuss those options after I look at the books."

Buzzing hummed in Hank's ears. He shook his head, but it only grew louder.

He couldn't stop. He *needed* to know. *Now.*

"Tell me," he insisted, grinding it out between clenched teeth while panic rose like bile into his throat. This was what he'd always feared, wasn't it? That he would screw up so badly he would lose everything that mattered to him.

"If we have to," Amy whispered, "we would sell the ranch."

The pronouncement bounced from the walls. It shot through the buzzing in his ears.

Hank sat in the eerie silence that followed and felt his heart fall through his body to the floor.

Sell the ranch.

The very worst the world could dish out.

But things weren't that bad. *Why* would Leila and this woman think they could be?

Anger blazed through him, and the buzzing returned with a roar.

"Come again?" Hank yelled at the pale woman on the sofa.

The knuckles of Amy's clenched hands turned white in her lap. "Leila is afraid that selling the ranch might be the only option."

"You can't—" His jaw tightened. "You wouldn't—"

"I'm just preparing you for the worst." Amy's voice was gentle again, but it tore through Hank's skin. Like thistledown coating barbed wire, it did nothing to ease his pain.

"But things aren't that bad. Donna at the bank would have warned me," Hank insisted, his heart pounding his ribs.

"Because of the letter Leila received, she seems to think they are. We have to consider all options."

Hank couldn't figure out what was going on here. He'd been so careful.

Leila was making a mistake. This woman shouldn't be here, talking about worst-case scenarios. He surged out of his chair.

No, he refused to accept this.

Hank pointed a finger Amy's way and raised his voice. "Maybe where you come from, people consider all options, but in these parts, we don't consider options we don't believe in." The pain of his unruly emotions, and his shame, and his fear of his own incompetence built in his chest. "We work hard to keep what's ours."

He towered over her and, for the briefest moment, she shrank against the back of the couch.

Then, her green eyes glittered with defiance, like she was building her own head of steam, and she sat up straight. One cheek turned pink, only one, fascinating him. It was the damnedest thing to watch that cheek turn even redder, while the other stayed pale. *Peculiar.* Another of those words he loved.

Forget the damn words you love!

She was casting a spell over him. Was this how she worked? Pulling men into some kind of obsession? Damned if he'd let her.

He felt the heat and anger of his own helplessness, at his own lack of control over the ranch he'd grown up on and loved, steamroll over this petite, dangerously beautiful woman.

"You'll sell this ranch over my dead body," he hollered.

He turned and stormed from the room, only to draw up short. Willie was herding the children out of the dining room into the hall and toward the front door. They stared at Hank with wide eyes.

His gut churned. He'd *never* raised his voice in front of any child before.

He rushed from the house and raced across the yard to the stable.

CHAPTER THREE

AMY STARED at his retreating back. The man wasn't as mild-mannered as he looked.

The counselors began to herd the children through the front door.

"Take them to the field and start a game," Willie said. The counselors nodded.

Willie walked to where she sat on the sofa.

"He has a temper," she said, glancing at him for confirmation, but the ranch foreman looked at her as if she'd crawled out from under a rock.

"That there," he said, leaning toward her, "is the first time I've seen that boy lose his temper since he was sixteen."

He smacked his dirty hat onto his gray hair and pinned Amy with shrewd eyes. He got close enough for her to smell coffee on his breath. "You couldn'a picked a better way to make an enemy of the sweetest boy on the face of this earth."

He left the room, the heels of his cowboy boots banging reproach on the floor of the hall.

Amy sat dazed.

She'd seen the censure of every child and teenager standing in the hall when Hank had stormed out. Rather than blame him for his bad behavior, they'd looked at her as if she were the one at fault.

She raised her hand to her hot cheek, thinking of the way Hank had looked at her a few moments ago, not with the heat of anger, but with something almost like hunger. Then rage had taken its place, all of it directed at her.

The commingled heat of anger and chagrin burned through her.

How dare Hank make her look bad in front of these children?

Two years ago, she would have found a way to handle the situation better, but she was so far off her stride these days. Why hadn't Leila warned Hank about this option? Perhaps she'd been wary of Hank's reaction and had left it for Amy to deal with. So odd for take-charge Leila.

Amy stood and walked to her room, where she sat on her bed and fumed. How dare he treat her as if *she* was the villain here? *He'd* gotten himself into financial trouble, not *her*.

She had a good mind to march right back home to Billings and leave the ornery man to deal with his own problems.

Him and his useless pride. Over the past ten years, she'd often run into foolish pride in mismanaged corporations. Boards and managers who called on her for help routinely ignored her hard-won reputation and refused to consider her solutions.

Stubborn, stubborn man. Did Hank think she would be here if the situation wasn't dire? Did he think übercapable Leila panicked at the drop of a hat?

And Willie. Did he have to look at *her* as if *she* was the cause of their problems?

She knew what would come next on Hank's part—resistance, sly questions about her competence, the insistence on a second opinion. All in all, a noxious brew that wouldn't let up until she either saved the ranch for them, or sold it.

She rubbed her temples. She was so darn tired of fighting, and she wasn't sure she had the patience left to help people who wouldn't help themselves.

The hell with it.

She was leaving.

She picked up her purse and dragged her suitcase from the bed.

As she reached the door, an image of Leila's worried face popped into her mind. Leila had been her rock for the past two years. Amy owed her big-time and didn't resent the debt one iota.

She sighed. Of course she wouldn't leave. One more image of Leila's normally indomitable face creased with worry was enough to make Amy stay put.

More importantly, if Amy went home, she would be back to square one. Living like a hermit. Ignoring decisions that needed to be made about her business. Wallowing in self-pity.

Leila hadn't asked Amy to come. Amy had volunteered, both for her friend and for herself.

It was time to get over her problems and get on with life. These children could help her.

She set down her bags, walked to the window and stared at the massive fields of waving grain, at the neat-as-a-pin grounds, and at the large solid buildings—stables, barns, garages—all white and red in the blazing sun. Not one sign of neglect.

Admittedly Hank took care of the place.

In one of the fenced corrals, a mother horse and her baby nuzzled noses. Colt? Calf? No, calves were cows. Weren't they?

This ranch could help her.

She'd stay.

For one week.

Not one day longer.

If an accountant with her skills couldn't set this place right in a week, then it was time to change careers.

Amy took a deep, sustaining breath and turned from the window. She needed to call her mother, who would fret until she heard from Amy.

She pulled her cell phone from her purse and dialed the number in Billings.

"Hello?" Mother's voice quavered more with each passing week.

"Hi, it's me."

"I was expecting you to call a long time ago, you know?" Rarely did her mother make a statement that didn't end with a question mark. Maybe the habit came from watching *Jeopardy!* every night for twenty years.

"Yes, I know, but it was a long drive then I had lunch."

"When are you coming home, dear?"

Amy sighed. She'd already told Mother a number of times she'd be here until she solved the problem. If Mother had Alzheimer's or dementia, Amy could understand her behavior. But Amy knew this was an attempt to make her feel guilty about leaving Billings.

She also knew how lonely Mother was.

Caught in a bind between impatience and love, she asked, "Have you gone to any of those socials your church organizes?"

"No. I don't know anyone there, do I?"

"That is the point of the socials. To get to know other people."

"But I don't know anyone *now,* do I? So I would have to make new friends. That's hard for me, you know?"

Amy counted to ten. *Oh, Mother, darling, get a life.*

The silence stretched until her mother broke it. "When are you coming home?"

"I'll come back on the weekend for a visit. I'll stay with you on Saturday night. How does that sound?"

"Today is only Monday," Mother said, a thread of desperation running through her tone. "Saturday is a long way away. Can you come on Friday night?"

Amy squeezed the top of her nose to ease a building headache.

"Yes. I'll see you at dinnertime."

She closed her phone with a click and sat with her eyes closed. When had the child become the parent and her mother, the child?

She opened her purse and took out the small jade cat she carried everywhere. Her dad had given it to her after her pet, Princie, had been hit by a car. It sat in her hand, cool and green.

"She's the exact shade of your pretty green eyes," he'd said. "This little cat will never die. She'll be your friend forever."

That day, she'd felt nothing could harm her while Dad was around.

She set the cat on the bedside table and pushed away those memories.

Enough. No dwelling on pain or death.

Instead, figure out what you plan to do about this ranch.

And what you plan to do about Hank Shelter. She had a bone to pick with him.

He owed her for embarrassing her in front of everyone. She'd wait until the time was right then let him have it, full blast, both barrels blazing.

Images of his sweet smile and the sensitive way he played with the children flashed through her mind, and she hesitated, but the memory of him towering over her and yelling at her won out.

Hank Shelter deserved a set down, and she was just the person to administer it.

HANK PACED the length of the stable's center aisle from front to back and back to front again.

Time to be honest with himself. This whole situation rattled him. *She* rattled him. He remembered the way he'd stood over Amy, trying to make her take back what she'd said about selling the ranch. He never used his size to intimidate people, 'specially not women or children.

Whether or not the bank said there was nothing wrong, she and Leila could sell the ranch out from under him and he wouldn't have a speck of power to prevent it.

He pounded his fist against the wall.

"Damn you, Dad. It should have been mine."

Hank knew the truth, though, knew exactly why Dad hadn't left the ranch to him, and he hung his head, choked by shame. Once that woman got to the books, she would know, too. In a matter of time, the whole world would.

He leaned his forehead on the rough wood and breathed heavily, hot air hitting the wall and bouncing back to bathe his face. He'd lived with his problem all his life. He would live with it for the rest, but Lord help him, he needed to do it here, on this ranch, where he felt strong and capable. And of value.

The sound of his fist hitting the wall again reverberated in the cavernous room.

Stop, he warned himself. *Pull yourself together.*

No. He wasn't losing this land that was more precious to him than his own life. He was not abandoning those kids, who needed this place with every breath they took.

He threw back his head and yelled, "I'm not leaving this ranch!"

"That's the spirit."

Hank spun around at the sound of Willie's voice. The older man stood silhouetted in the open doorway of the building. Was it a trick of the sun that made him look shorter? Willie stepped into the cool interior and Hank noticed for the first time how stooped his foreman was becoming.

"Feel any better after that outburst?" Willie's

tone held reproach. He walked closer and stood with arms akimbo.

Hank ran his fingers through his hair and his anger abated. "Can't believe I got mad enough to yell where the children would hear me."

"I think the next county heard you," Willie said. "Haven't seen that since you started bringing the children here." Willie's voice wavered, thinner than it used to be. A lot of things were thinner about Willie these days. He was getting old. Hank would have to lay him off if he lost the ranch. Where on earth would Willie go at his age?

Hank would lose the best friend he'd ever had. He'd had a stronger connection with the foreman than he'd ever had with his own father.

Nope. Wasn't about to happen. He was losing neither the ranch nor Willie.

"If things got really bad, we might have to sell."

Willie dropped his arms to his sides. "It's that close?"

"I don't know." Hank scuffed a boot in the dirt. "I kind of forced her to tell me the worst that could happen."

Dust motes drifted in a sunbeam that shone through a high window.

Willie set his foot on a bale of straw and rested his elbow on his knee. "Sounds like you aren't gonna take this sitting down."

"I plan to fight back," Hank answered.

Willie's white mustache curled up at the corners. He looked at Hank with gray eyes. "Glad to hear you say that."

"I shouldn't have made a scene in front of the kids."

"Nope. But you did, so move on. Should have a little talk with them. Reassure them everything's all right."

Hank nodded. "Yeah. I'll do that." He straightened. "Now."

Funny how the sound of those kids chattering across the yard gave him hope. When they'd gotten here two weeks ago, they'd been the saddest, quietest bunch of tots he'd seen in an age.

"Can you help Haley and Rich watch the children for a while?" Hank asked.

"Sure can. Whatcha have in mind to do?"

"I'm going to keep her out of that office," Hank said.

"You sure that's wise? Why not let her in and get it over with?"

Hank shrugged. "Just can't let her in there."

"Don't forget, you catch more flies with honey." Willie laughed. "Sweeten her up."

Hank smiled and it felt strained. He knew kids. He didn't much know women.

Time to learn.

Fast.

He stepped into the sun-drenched yard and spotted the children in the field on the other side of the corral. He joined them there.

"Kids," he said as they swarmed him, clutching his arms, sitting on his feet, wrapping arms around his waist. "I got to give y'all an apology. I shouldn't have yelled at that lady like that."

Cheryl's solemn gaze disconcerted him. She was the most fragile of the group and the wisest— an old woman in a child's body. She raised her arms to be lifted.

He picked her up and settled her against his chest.

"Don't be mad," she whispered.

"I'm not mad, darlin', not anymore," he said.

Nope, not mad. Determined.

As AMY WALKED across the yard, she watched Hank talk to the girl with the haunting eyes. Looked like there was some kind of bond between them.

She wouldn't let sentiment overcome her resolve, though.

"We need to talk," she said as she approached. She nodded her head toward the children, who watched her warily. "Privately."

Hank put down the girl. She and the other children ran to the counselors in the field.

"I'd like to see the office," Amy said.

Hank cracked the knuckles of his left hand. He frowned intensely, like he was thinking hard about something, then his face lit up.

"Hungry Hollow!" he shouted, then lowered his voice. "You need to see the neighboring ranch."

"Later. I really think—"

"It's the *working* part of this property."

That stopped her even more than the cunning look in his eye. The working part would be important. She had to get to those books, though.

"But—"

"It brings in a good income," he said.

Okay, she would need to know how Hank supported this whole operation. She nodded. "I should check it out."

"Yeah, we can ride over."

"Ride? On a horse?" She placed a hand against her chest, then dropped it the second she realized it drew his eyes to her body.

"I'll drive over," she said, "and meet you there."

"No need. We can take the pickup truck if you don't want to ride."

"No," she said, her voice shaky. "I'd rather not ride." *Not on your life.*

Half an hour later, Amy sat in Hank's dusty black pickup, checking out the details of this man's life. A crack in the upholstery had been repaired with duct tape, gray against the black. In contrast, a top-of-the-line CD player shone through a coat of dust on the dashboard.

Amy noticed the cover of an audio book on the dashboard: Stephen Hawking's *A Brief History of Time*. Wow, heavy reading. Amy had tried it once and hadn't had the patience for it.

A *rancher* listening to Hawking? Hank?

Okay, Amy, back off on the prejudices.

As the truck bumped along, Amy felt like a sack of turnips, tossed around by the ruts of Hungry Hollow's driveway.

Hank's hand on the gearshift brushed her knee. The man radiated heat like an oven. Her fingers hurt from gripping the door handle to stay on her side of the truck, and still she could feel his heat.

It felt too good.

"I need to apologize to you for yelling," Hank said above the noise of the truck as he geared down. "I don't normally do that."

"So Willie led me to believe." Amy knew she sounded cool but didn't care. The man had been unreasonable.

Hank nodded.

A bag of candy in the cup holder caught her eye and she picked it up. "Humbugs," she cried.

"Yep. They're my favorite." Hank looked her way. "You like them?"

"I love them, but I don't see them very often."

"Help yourself. I get them in Ordinary, in a

shop called Sweet Talk." Hank steered the truck onto a dirt road with a house in the distance.

"You should take a drive into Ordinary," he said. "It's a real sweet little town, the lifeline for all of us ranchers in the district."

Amy doubted she'd make it into town during this short visit. It had nothing to do with her job here.

After circling into the yard of a big old brick farmhouse, they pulled up in front of a corral teeming with men, horses and dust.

Amy felt the truck dip and lift as Hank stepped out, yelling, "Hey, Angus. What's up?"

Angus, a dark-haired, fortysomething man with enough character in his face to make it more than handsome, shook Hank's hand and swatted him on the arm loudly enough for Amy to hear from the open passenger window. Hank didn't budge an inch. He tapped Angus on the shoulder, raising a cloud of dust from his shirt.

"The boys are practicing for the rodeo," Angus said. "You here to do some bronc-bustin'?"

"Naw, not today. I'm just showing my guest around."

Amy stepped out of the truck with her notebook in hand.

"Amy," Hank said, "this is my neighbor, Angus Kinsey, from the Circle K on the other side of the Sheltering Arms. Angus, this is Amy Graves."

Angus had a good, strong handshake, and a set of admiring eyes. They felt good on her. Amy smiled.

She wandered with the two men to the corral fence.

Hank leaned his arms across the top as more men congregated outside the corral, leaving a couple of men inside standing beside a small horse. None of them seemed to notice Amy, which was fine with her. She was here to observe them and the way things were done around here.

"So," she asked, "you raise horses at Hungry Hollow?"

Hank turned her way. "Everyone around here owns and raises horses." He shrugged. "They're part of the ranching life."

"Are they like cows? You raise them for their meat?"

Both Angus and Hank looked at her strangely. Amy wondered about the crafty gleam in Hank's eye.

"No, we don't sell horses for meat—" Angus would have said more, but Hank cut him off.

"We raise them for glue."

Glue, my rear end, she thought. *You're making fun of the city slicker. Two can play that game.* She flipped open her notebook and retrieved a pen from her pocket.

"How much do you get per horse? Do you sell

them by the pound? What part produces glue?"
She shivered—it was a gory subject—but if Hank
wanted to make a mockery of this visit, she'd ac-
commodate him.

It was Hank's turn to stare at her with his jaw
gaping. His dark brown eyes widened.

She grinned, meanly, and said, "Gotcha."

Angus laughed and slapped Hank's back.

"Seriously," she said, glad to have rattled him,
"do you raise the horses to sell?"

"The truth is," Hank said in a chagrined voice,
"we raise most of our horses to work, but we also
keep a special set for rodeo."

The horse in the center of the corral whickered
and tried to pull away from the cowboy who was
restraining him, but the man held on tight.

Hank nodded toward the horse. "That looks
like the Circle K's Rusty."

"It is," Angus said.

"He's a mean one." Hank sounded anything
but stern. He sounded proud. "Who's getting up
on him first?"

"Heel."

"That the new guy?"

"Yup."

"Let's see what he can do." Hank leaned
forward, his body straining toward the action on
the other side of the fence.

When the rider mounted the horse, Amy

watched a flash of excitement light Hank's face. The men started to cheer. The rider held on to the reins with one hand as the horse bucked and reared, trying to unseat him.

"That's a chiropractor's worst nightmare," Amy shouted above the roar of the men, shaking her head.

Hank looked at her, his sparkling eyes alight with fun, like a kid's.

Amy noticed all the men looked like a bunch of overgrown, overexcited boys.

Heel flew from the horse, slamming to the ground in a cloud of dust, and all the men groaned. In a split second, he was on his feet, cursing, then laughing, retrieving his hat and setting it back onto his head. Tough guy.

"Exhilarating," Hank murmured.

"We should look at the rest of the ranch now," Amy said, leaning close to Hank.

He nodded but didn't answer, keeping his gaze on the horse.

One of the cowboys got the bronc back under control. "You want to try him next?" Angus asked Hank.

Hank set one hand on top of the chest-high fence, one foot on the second rail, and vaulted over it, looking like a six-year-old who'd gotten his first pair of skates for Christmas.

"Hey, we're supposed to be here on business,"

Amy called, but he either didn't hear her or chose to ignore her.

The bronco stood with his legs locked while Hank mounted him. As the horse reared, Hank held on to the reins with one hand, and let the other arm fly straight and high above his head.

The horse bucked.

Amy expected him to fall off. He didn't. She held her breath.

"Hoooooeeeee," one of the cowboys sang.

"Ride him, Hank," another yelled.

Amy watched his muscular body get tossed around like a feather on the horse's back, and she felt a stirring of fear in her belly.

Hank anticipated the horse's every move, his big thighs gripping the animal's sides. The horse dipped, he dipped. The horse reared, he followed, his expression fierce.

In spite of herself, Amy watched in fascination. Excitement replaced her fear.

As the crowd cheered and the bronco's hooves pounded, Hank jumped from the animal's back. The bronc ran to the opposite side of the corral, then stood with sides heaving like leathery bellows.

Amy stared at Hank. He seemed barely winded. Picking up his dirty white Stetson from the dry ground, he rapped it against his thigh and set it on his head, a broad grin creasing his face.

Her knees got weak. There he went again with that magical smile.

Hank crossed the corral toward Amy, his stride long and confident—in his element, like a cowboy of old, taming beasts and all obstacles.

When he looked at her, Hank's step faltered. He stared at her with a heat that might, just might, match her own.

When he reached her, he leaned close and whispered, "You okay?"

The men in the corral and lining the fence turned as one to watch her. Amy stared back. Young and old, tall and short, handsome and homely, every one of them had one thing in common with Hank— a lean, stringy strength earned through hard labor.

They surrounded her, nudging Hank out of the way, all speaking at once.

"Well, look here."

"You new to these parts?"

"Hey, ma'am, I'm Ash."

"Aren't you a beauty?"

Did people really say those things in the twenty-first century? Still, in spite of their testosterone-driven competition and manly posturing to get her attention, these men charmed her.

Then Hank gripped her elbow hard and pulled her toward the truck.

"But, I—" She peered over her shoulder at the men who smiled and waved to her.

"We have to get back to those kids," he grumbled.

She resisted his pull. "But I—"

"We're out of time. Need to get home."

Amy dug in her heels. "We're here to check out the business. I'm not leaving until we do."

CHAPTER FOUR

"WHOA, HANK," Angus called. "Not so fast. If Ms. Graves wants to hang out for a while, we'd be happy to entertain her." He approached, took Amy's elbow and led her toward the corral.

Angus's eyes sparkled when he looked down at Amy. She smiled up at him.

Hank choked. For a peace-loving man, which he most certainly was, he was strongly tempted to rearrange Angus's charming face.

"I'm about ready to practice my rope tricks," young Ty Walker yelled from across the yard, his smile wide and hokey. "Amy can watch."

Someone should tell him he looks goofy when he smiles like that, Hank thought. Like a love-sick moose.

"I can drive her home later if you want, Hank," Hip said.

Over my dead body, Hank thought, and stood beside Amy.

Ty picked up a rope and tied a honda, then passed the plain end through the honda to make a loop. He started to spin it nice and slow. Like any cowboy worth his salt, he spun and worked the rope to an impressive four-foot loop, which he tossed over his head and down his body until it spun around his waist.

Ty smiled his goofy grin while he watched Amy. She clapped and laughed, her pretty smile sparkling in the sun.

Angus put a hand on her shoulder, a hand that would be broken in about two seconds if he wasn't careful. Hank's mind was turning to violence at every turn.

"That's called a body spin, but the prettier term is wedding ring," Angus said.

Amy nodded and smiled at him.

Hip ran forward with a rope of his own.

"Watch this, Amy." Hip started spinning a flat loop in front of his body. When he'd worked the rope to a good-size loop he passed it to his right hand and around his back, picking it up with his other hand and bringing it around front again on the other side.

"That's a merry-go-round," Angus said.

Hip threw the loop high over his head and kept spinning it. "Look, Amy," he shouted.

Hip was a good twenty years older than Amy. Disgusting way for a middle-aged man to behave in front of a young woman.

Show off. *Braggart.* Good word.

A split second before Hip threw the loop toward Amy, Hank realized his intention and spun Amy around out of the way, then pulled her flush against his chest, but Hip was too fast and his aim too accurate.

The loop settled over Amy, but also caught Hank, the rope tightening around them with the gentle persuasion of a mare nudging her colt home.

Hank heard shouts and whoops of laughter from the men, and heard Angus say, "Nice hoolihan, Hip," but all Hank saw was Amy.

She'd raised her arms when he'd pulled her toward him and her hands rested high on his chest. They rose and fell with his quick breaths, branding him.

The sounds around him drifted away. He lost himself in Amy's green eyes.

His hands held the back of her waist, drifted down to her hips. He thought of ripe pears and his blond guitar.

She smelled warm, like the sun, like mango and papaya and coconut.

Her skin looked soft enough to lick.

What if he did what he wanted and rested his head on her golden hair, felt the glide of it across his cheek?

What if he pressed his lips to her eyelids to close them, so she couldn't see all those handsome cowboys crowding around her? What if he kissed her until she was aware of only plain Hank?

Before he could act on the crazy impulse, she did the oddest thing. She closed her eyes and leaned forward, then smelled him with a delicate sniff.

She opened her eyes and smiled into his. "Soap. Nice."

When she raised her hands to his shoulders, his arms automatically drew her closer, until her chest was flush against his.

She stiffened. Then, as if he'd doused a roaring fire, she grew icy. Her skin paled. Her lips thinned. The light in her emerald eyes died.

She dropped her gaze to his chest and one cheek burned red, and he could swear she was more than just turning cold on him. She was ashamed about something.

What the heck?

He felt a tug on the rope and realized Hip was gathering it up, forming loops over the fingers of one hand. Hank shook himself out of his stupor and turned to the old ranch hand.

"Hip," he said, "you could have hurt Amy."

Hip slowed his approach, his expression sheepish. "Aw, Hank, you know I'd never hurt a woman. Been doing these tricks since I was eight years old."

He lifted the loop above Hank's and Amy's heads as carefully as if she were a skittish horse. Hank felt reluctant contrition about his behavior toward Hip—*contrition,* great word—but then Amy smiled, rose on tiptoes and kissed Hip's cheek.

Hank had the urge to rub a little dirt in the guy's face, even if Hip was an older man.

Hank stalked to the truck, ashamed of his nasty urges. What the *heck* was wrong with him? He wasn't a violent man.

"Amy," he called, his tone brooking no opposition. "We need to go."

She didn't reply.

"Now," he said.

Nothing was going to happen with this woman.

Amy ran to the truck and jumped in, but she didn't look happy about it. She didn't say a word about checking out the business.

He steered the truck toward the Sheltering Arms, heading out across fields instead of down the driveway to the road.

AMY WAS STILL having trouble catching her breath after being crowded against Hank's big body. His very hard, muscular body.

He'd felt so good she'd wanted to stay there for days, staring into his laughing brown eyes, feeling his heat spread through her.

Then her traitorous arms had slid a path up to his shoulders and he'd pulled her close until her chest hit his. Oh, that horrible moment when she'd wondered if he knew, if he could feel how she differed from a normal woman.

Could the day possibly get any more rocky?

Maybe tomorrow, after a good night's sleep, would be a better time to deal with business.

The truck lurched as Hank swung it around in the yard. Amy fell hard against him. He pushed her upright with a gentle hand. "You should put your seat belt on."

"Sorry, I forgot," she mumbled as she slid over to lean against the passenger door, then pulled the harness across her body.

She bumped against the handle as the truck bounced over a rut, and her mind finally registered that they were driving over fields instead of to the small highway leading back to the ranch.

"Where are we going?" she asked.

Hank pushed his hat back and wiped his forehead. "I want to see if we can catch sight of the campers."

"Campers?" Amy asked, curious in spite of herself.

"The little kids you met aren't the only ones we have at the ranch right now. The five older ones headed out this morning for a camping trip on Hungry Hollow land."

"Who went with them? More counselors?"

"A bunch of my ranch hands."

"Why would they camp over here? Why not on Sheltering Arms land?"

"I want them to see what goes on at a real working ranch. Most of these kids have never seen a steer in their lives."

Suddenly he pointed to a cloud of dust on the horizon and gunned the engine. "There."

When they flew over a hill and landed in a small gully on the far side of it, Amy's jaw snapped shut. She braced one hand against the door and one against the dashboard. Her butt hurt from bouncing on the firm seat.

She glanced at Hank. He was barely aware of the bumps. His mustache curved up at the ends, echoing a smile on his lips. Damp hair stuck out under the brim of his hat, punctuated by the caramel streak at his widow's peak.

As they approached the cloud, his grin broadened.

Amy watched dust swirl around a small herd of cows, or steers, or whatever they were, thirty yards away. Cowboys on nimble horses raced around the edges, controlling where the cows went. Mooing and yelling and rumbling hooves drowned out everything else. The pickup got close before she realized the ranch hands had children on their saddles in front of them while they herded cattle.

Dear God, were they crazy? Her heart pounded.

"Those children will fall off," Amy cried.

She unsnapped her seat belt and threw her door open.

"Hey!" Hank yelled. "You can't go out there."

She was half out of the truck when Hank wrapped his fingers around her arm and hauled her back in.

"Are you nuts?"

She sucked in a breath and ran a shaky hand over her face.

"I'm sorry," she said. Her voice trembled.

Hank reached across her, his big chest crushing her against the back of the seat and closed her door.

His dark eyes sparked fire.

"What the hell were you thinking?" His voice boomed in the close interior of the truck. "What were you going to do? Run into a herd of cattle?"

"I'm sorry," she whispered again, wondering at the strength of his reaction.

She touched his arm with one damp palm. "I'm afraid the children will fall. They'll get hurt."

His expression eased. His lips softened. "They're fine," he said.

Tears welled in Amy's eyes and she turned away so he wouldn't see. "They'll get hurt. Stop them. *Please*."

"Hey, it's okay." When she turned to him to

object, he raised his hand to stall her. "Those kids are safe with the ranch hands. Most of my workers have been on horses since they were two years old." He smiled. "Some of them ride better than they walk."

"But—"

"This isn't a real roundup, anyway. It's just a little one staged for the kids."

"Even so—"

When she reached for the door handle, still foolishly tempted to get out and rescue those children, Hank touched her shoulder to press her back against the seat.

"Sit and watch for a minute." His quiet tone eased some of her fear.

Hank pointed to the nearest man. "See?"

Sure enough, the cowboy had a forearm as lean and strong as one of Hank's wrapped around a boy's waist. As Amy watched, he controlled the horse with his strong thighs and with the reins he held in his other hand.

The boy's face practically glowed with excitement. He yelled at the horses, at the other cowboys, at the cattle. Directing them. As one of the animals broke out of the pack, he shouted, "Get him!" to the cowboy.

The cowboy laughed and yelled, "Sure, boss."

The vibration of the herd's frenetic motion rumbled through the truck. Leaning forward,

Amy peered through the dust, trying to spot more children. Each one reflected that same joyous expression.

With her hands pressing hard on her thighs, Amy forced herself to calm down.

She turned to Hank to apologize, but the words froze on her tongue. He was resting his forearms on the steering wheel, his body straining forward. His eyes followed every bit of the action.

He wants to be out there in the thick of it all.

"Do you ever do this with the kids?" she asked.

He fell back against the seat and straightened his hat on his head.

"Yeah. We take turns going on the overnight trips. I'll do the next batch of kids who come to the ranch. Just the older ones."

He pinned her with a piercing look. "When you first got here this morning, I thought you didn't like the kids."

She didn't answer. How could she ever make him understand how deeply her fears ran? How hard it was for her to care for people she might lose?

"Now I'm thinking maybe you're afraid of them," he continued. "Or afraid *for* them."

The man saw too much. He leaned against his door and studied her. The cab of the truck became a cocoon, enveloping Amy in a potent blend of fright, compassion and a desire to confess.

Her pulse pounded in her ears. "My father died when I was fourteen. In front of me. Heart attack. I couldn't save him."

She stared out the window and swallowed hard. "It left me terrified of bad things happening to people." She'd never discussed this phobia with anyone before.

"All right," Hank said. "I can understand that."

She had no doubt that he could.

The cowboy with the excited boy on his lap rode up to the truck, on Amy's side. He leaned down from his horse and pressed his hand into Amy's.

"Hi," he said. "I'm Matt." He had a smile that could dazzle, and he knew it.

"I'm Amy," she said.

Hank said, "Matt," and his dry tone had Matt looking at him then laughing, as if he knew a secret about Hank.

Matt said, "This here's Davey."

Amy smiled at the boy. They smelled like hay and horses and a touch of manure. Matt's horse whinnied, clearly wanting to get back to work, but Matt held him steady.

"You here for the day?" Matt asked.

"No," Amy said. "I'm here for the rest of the week. At the Sheltering Arms."

"Well, then, I'll be seeing you in a couple of days." He doffed his hat and nodded. "How 'bout we get to know each other better then?"

He turned his horse and rode away.

Matt wasn't her type at all, but she gave him points for trying.

Putting the truck into gear, Hank headed in a direction Amy guessed would take them to the Sheltering Arms.

The practical accountant in her broke the silence. "You know you're just asking for a lawsuit if one of those kids gets hurt."

"They won't."

"What if one of them does? Any of those children could get sick again. Are you qualified to deal with that?"

"Uh-huh. We all have first-aid training."

"I think it should go further than that. Some of those children must still be taking medications. I would almost want to see a nurse living at the ranch."

"There is a full-time nurse at the ranch," Hank said, a sly glimmer of humor in his eyes.

"Who?"

"Hannah." Hank grinned.

"The housekeeper?" Amy spluttered.

"Yup. She offered to train when I decided to bring children to the ranch fifteen years ago."

Okay, that surprised her. Hannah probably already had a heavy load to carry running that house, yet she cared enough to become a nurse.

Amy had to stop underestimating these people.

"You got to understand what's important here." He pulled his gaze away from the field in front of them. "The kids are what's important, and giving them the fullest experience here they can possibly have."

He faced forward again. "Because they deserve it after all they've lived through."

With those words, a heaviness hung in the air between them.

"Why did you turn the ranch into a place for cancer survivors?" she asked.

"I—" Hank's face was suddenly neutral, as unresponsive as Amy had seen it.

She held her breath.

"I had a son. He died of leukemia when he was two."

"I'm so sorry," she whispered. Dear God, his son. *His* son. "So sorry."

He whispered one word, little more than a sigh, but she was pretty sure it was "Jamie."

She hitched a breath. Knowing his name made the child too real to her.

Swallowing her cowardice, she asked, "Do you want to talk about him?" And prayed that he wouldn't.

He shook his head.

Her relief stunned her. She couldn't imagine his pain, didn't know what to say. She remained silent for the rest of the ride home.

As they neared the house, she stole a glimpse at him. His jaw was hard, his mouth thin. Then he saw the children on the veranda. The sight smoothed the worry lines from his brow, softened his full lips, turned up the corners of his mouth.

When they parked, the younger children ran across the lawn to greet him. Four of them crowded his door.

"Hey, back up, hooligans," Hank said, back to his cheerful self, as if the children gave him a deeper perspective on life. It was clear they set everything into place in Hank's world.

Amy stared at him, amazed by the change.

"How's a cowboy supposed ta get out of his truck?" he asked, using the fake cowboy accent she'd noticed he put on for the kids.

When Amy stepped out on the passenger side, the solemn young girl stood waiting for her, her eyes big. She placed her hand into one of Amy's and held on.

As though Amy's fingers had a mind of their own, they curled around the tiny hand. Amy stared down at her and swallowed hard, forcing herself to stay put. Such honest trust, given so freely.

As they walked around the front of the pickup, Amy wondered what on earth the child saw in her that made her want to get close. Amy had so little to offer others these days.

She wanted to tell the girl not to depend on her, that Amy didn't get close to people.

She looked away, unable to withstand the child's intense gaze. And yet she still held her hand.

Hank lifted a small girl and threw her above his head into the air. Amy gasped, but Hank caught the giggling child on the way down.

"Do me, Hank. Do me," begged a young boy with skin the color of coffee with cream. Hank tossed the boy into the air and his biceps bulged against the plaid cotton of his shirtsleeves.

He threw every child into the air who asked for it, as many times as they asked. Even when the underarms of his shirt showed big damp circles and a sheen of sweat coated his brow, he didn't stop until the last kid had wheedled for a toss.

Amy wondered at the resiliency of this man and realized that he drew it directly from these children.

"Hey," he said, sounding only barely winded, "what did the horse say when the kid from the next ranch came to visit?"

"What, Hank?" they chimed.

"Howdy, *nei-ei-ei-ei-gh-gh-gh-gh-bor.*"

Amy rolled her eyes. He had to be kidding. Did he really think that was funny?

The kids laughed. Apparently it didn't take much to entertain a child.

"You people plumb wear me out," Hank said.

Watching the children's faces, Amy noticed they fell for his shtick hook, line and sinker. They loved it. They loved Hank.

He collapsed onto the grass in front of the house, with kids falling all over him. The solemn girl let go of Amy's hand and joined the others.

Amy stared at her empty hand, suddenly cool after losing the child's warmth. Then she looked at Hank, covered by miniature candles of hope lighting the darkness of a harsh world, and she knew why he did this. He needed those children as much as they needed him.

It didn't seem to take much to make him happy—horses, cows, dust and kids.

Watching him, Amy felt a pang of envy. What would it take to make her happy? Peace on earth? Certainly. No such thing as death? Yes many times over. To be happy and excited about her work again? Yes. Her husband back in her arms? Maybe not.

That answer surprised her. A month ago, she would have answered with a resounding "yes."

Bemused, she headed for the house.

AFTER LEAVING the children in the kitchen with Hannah, Hank walked toward the three-car garage across from the largest stable. Thinking about his son always left him melancholy, in spite of the fun he'd just had with the children. Lord, he missed Jamie.

Willie lived in an apartment on the second floor, with blue window boxes that the man himself had filled with red geraniums and white alyssum.

Hank needed to talk to Willie, to make sense of his conflicting feelings about that woman.

He climbed the stairs, knocked, then walked into a home as spotless as a Betty Crocker test kitchen. Willie's fastidiousness always took Hank by surprise.

"Willie," he called. "You here?"

Willie stepped out of his bedroom buttoning up a clean denim shirt, covering the fuzz of gray hair on his chest.

"How'd the trip to the ranch go?" he asked, tucking the shirt into his pants.

"Good," Hank said. "You got any coffee on?"

Willie poured him a cup and handed it to him black.

Hank took a sip. "She…ah…she's a good person."

Willie's face registered surprise. "So you feel better about her now?"

"More sympathetic, I guess." Hank wandered to a window that faced the yard. "She's got a lot going on inside."

Maybe her vulnerability around the kids would work in his favor. Given her own shortcomings, she might be compassionate and forgiving once she saw the office. Was he willing to take that chance?

Aw hell, he needed her to see that there was no problem with the ranch. If he scooted her in there in the next day or two, maybe she could be finished by the end of the week, relieving him of this lump of dread in his stomach.

So what if she gave him a hard time about the state of his files? Embarrassment was a small price to pay for peace of mind.

Hank turned from the window and rubbed the back of his neck. "Listen, I'm going to let her see the books."

"Why?" Willie sipped his own coffee from a mug that read Bronc Riders Like To Buck.

"I need Amy to see that everything's okay with the finances, so she can go home and get Leila off my back."

Hank sat in a big armchair and balanced his cup on the arm.

"What if it turns out there really *is* something wrong with the ranch's finances? Something real bad?" The possibility made Hank shudder. "She'd have to find it 'cause I sure as heck couldn't."

"Makes sense, I guess," Willie said.

"Yeah. I'll get her to fix it then she can head home." He wanted her off the ranch before he cared for her even more than he did now.

"When?" Willie asked.

"When's she going home?"

"No. When are you unlocking the office for her?"

Hank stood, crossed to the kitchen and set his cup on the counter. "Tomorrow or the day after."

He turned to Willie, seeking approval of his plan. "Amy's gotta get emotionally invested in this place. I think I know how to do that."

"How?" Willie asked.

"I'm going to show her around the ranch before I open up the office to her. Let her see how much it means to the children." He drummed his fingers against his thigh. "I saw something in her today. She really likes kids. She cares about what happens to them."

"That's good." Willie nodded. "If she does find a problem, she'll be more likely to try to save the ranch than to sell it."

Hank filled with hope. "Exactly my thinking."

He rubbed his twitchy belly. He was banking a lot on being able to get the city woman to care about his ranch.

CHAPTER FIVE

THE FOLLOWING morning, Amy entered the dining room late for breakfast, head pounding from too little sleep, confused and groggy from yesterday's roller-coaster ride of emotions. Maybe she'd bitten off more than she could chew by coming here.

She rubbed her temples. She needed to get into the office to see what kind of challenges she faced there.

The dining room was empty. The children and Hank must already be outside working on the chores someone mentioned they did every day.

She stepped through a swinging door that led into the kitchen.

Light poured through numerous windows. Every spotless white cupboard, drawer, countertop and appliance contrasted against blue walls. The focal point was a huge, glossy oak plank table in the center of the room, where a small woman stood rolling out pastry.

Amy recognized Hannah, the housekeeper, by

Leila's description. So this little bird-boned woman was a nurse. More power to her.

Hannah looked up and smiled when she saw Amy.

"Morning," she said, then scuttled to the sink, as delicate as a sparrow and twice as quick.

She rinsed her hands and dried them, then turned back to Amy.

The wrinkles on Hannah's face created a network of enough complexity to put a map of New York City to shame. Her skin was not as darkly tanned as Hank's, but close. Amy bit her tongue to keep from telling her she should have used sunscreen over the years. Amy guessed her to be in her sixties, but the lines added years, as did the soft white hair.

Hannah smiled, sending a few rivers to criss-cross with a couple of mountain ranges, and waved Amy closer, then wrapped her arms around her. "Leila's friend Amy, so glad to meet you."

Amy strained against the contact, but found the woman's grip surprisingly strong, the meager bosom warm and her scent reminiscent of home in years long gone—of a vanilla and cinnamon essence that seemed to have taken root in the woman's pores. Amy stiffened against her own sentimentality.

Pulling out of the housekeeper's embrace, she said, "Hello, Hannah."

Hannah peered into Amy's eyes, then nodded. "We'll see what we can do for you here. This ranch, you know, it holds a lot of magic."

What had Hannah seen on Amy's face? What information was Amy unwittingly giving away about herself, making her too vulnerable?

Hannah bustled to the stove. "Hank, he keeps bringing the children here, and mostly they go home happy. You feel so good to help them. They laugh so much here."

Hannah spun around and handed Amy a bowl of oatmeal, then retrieved a carton of milk from the fridge. "Go into the dining room and eat."

Amy thanked her and left the kitchen. In the dining room, she fell into a chair to recover from the whirlwind that was Hannah. She sprinkled sugar on the glutinous gruel in her bowl and shrugged. Oatmeal was best served fresh. Her own fault for sleeping in.

After breakfast, she headed for the office but found the door locked.

She walked down the hall to search for Hank. Stepping onto the veranda, she saw no sign of him in the corrals or yard. Where was everyone? The heels of her sandals clicked on the gray wooden floor. She descended the steps.

A light June breeze carried the faint sounds of children's voices from the barn. It also held an elusive hint of fragrance from the garden. Funny that she hadn't noticed all these flowers yesterday.

She walked the length of the garden slowly, savoring the colors and scents.

"I can't do these up," a child's voice said from behind her.

Amy spun around.

The thin girl with the sallow skin stood behind her wearing a pair of overalls, but holding them up at the waist. Two straps trailed on the grass behind her.

Amy bent and picked up the straps, trying not to touch the narrow shoulders while buckling the straps to the bib. The child stared into her face, her eyes enormous.

"You're not doing chores," she accused.

Amy squirmed under the girl's steady gaze.

"We all got to do chores," the girl continued, her voice ripe with reproach.

Amy fought the guilt flooding her. She was here to do her own job. Wasn't that a chore?

Amy's braid fell over her shoulder and the child touched the end of it.

"Pretty," she murmured. "Can I get one of those when my hair grows back?"

Amy inhaled sharply. "Yes." The word whispered out of her.

"When?"

"Soon." Amy choked on the lie. It would take

a couple of years to grow her hair back as long as Amy's, but staring into the child's solemn blue eyes, she didn't have the heart to tell her so.

She stepped back from the girl. She couldn't do this.

Just as she turned away, the girl slipped her hand into Amy's. Amy curled her fingers around the tiny hand, then stared at it lying in her fist with a trust that humbled her.

Don't, she wanted to plead. *Don't rely on me. I don't know if I have anything to give you.*

But this was what she thought she'd wanted when she came here, wasn't it? Time to get on with life, she'd thought. What better way than trial by fire among these children? What a naive fool she'd been. The reality of this girl and her problems at such an early age broke Amy's heart.

"How old are you?" she asked.

The child turned her head on her scrawny neck to peer up at Amy.

"Six. How old are you?"

Old enough to be able to handle this, Amy thought, but she said aloud, "Thirty-one."

"What's your name?" the child asked.

"Amy."

"I'm Cheryl. That was Grandma's name."

Amy fought a fierce battle—to stay and learn more about this child who might die someday soon, or to run for the hills to bury herself in a cave. Alone.

Cheryl raised her arms to be picked up. Amy lifted the child, her actions unnatural, as though someone else held the strings that controlled her limbs. The girl was as light as a milkweed pod. Amy settled her onto her hip and tried to control the shaking in her knees.

Cheryl pointed to something under one of the plants. "What's that?"

Amy squatted, setting Cheryl on the grass beside her. Someone had tucked a clay toad house toward the back of the flower bed in the moist shade.

"A toad house." Amy cleared her throat of regret. "A toad will live here in the summer. Maybe there's already one inside."

Cheryl squatted beside her, with her hands curled over her knees. "What do they look like?"

Amy lifted the clay pot, but found nothing but damp soil underneath.

"They look like frogs, except they're larger and less green. They have a lot of different shades of brown on their bodies. So they can look like the soil."

"Why did Hannah give them a little house in her garden?"

Ah, so this was Hannah's garden.

"They eat all kinds of creatures who are hard on plants, who would try to eat Hannah's flowers," she said, surprised that the bits of knowledge her father had once shared with her came back. "Flies, bugs."

She'd forgotten about the small garden Dad had made for her behind their rental house.

Movement behind them startled both Amy and Cheryl. Hank's shadow covered them.

"I thought you were coming straight back to the stable from the washroom, Cheryl." His voice was starving for moisture this morning, like sandpaper on tree bark.

"Dragon scales," Cheryl said as she stared up at Hank.

Hank squatted in front of her. He snuggled her baseball cap more securely onto her head and tucked her shirt neatly into her overalls.

"What about dragon scales?" he asked.

"Your voice sounds like dragon scales. Rough."

"Rough, are they?"

Cheryl nodded. "And scaly."

Hank raised his thick eyebrows. "Dragon scales are scaly, are they?"

Cheryl nodded solemnly.

"And they sound like my voice?"

Cheryl bobbed her head. Hank wrapped his large hand around her tiny one and kissed her fingers.

"It's itchy." She pointed to his mustache.

"Like dragon scales?"

"Um…like…like…like snakeskin!"

Hank tickled her tummy. "You been kissing snakes lately?"

It was close, the tug at the corner of Cheryl's mouth. Almost a smile. Amy guessed the child didn't laugh very often. Hank picked her up and settled her onto his forearm, against his chest. She wrapped her thin arms around his neck.

"That's me, all right," he said. "Old snake-skinned, dragon-scaled Hank." He turned around and collided with Amy, obviously having forgotten she was there.

Amy watched a blush creep up Hank's neck and settle on his cheeks.

"I'm going to look for a toad in there every day." Cheryl pointed to the toad house.

"Is that right?" Hank asked.

It hurt to watch the affection between the two of them, the big cowboy and the fragile child. What if something happened to Hank? What if something happened to Cheryl?

"May I have the key to the office?" she blurted.

Hank's eyes widened at her abrupt tone. She moderated it. "I need to get started on those books."

She watched his Adam's apple bob. He glanced around, swiftly, as if looking for an escape route—or looking for a reason to keep her out of there.

"I think you should come in and go through them with me," she said.

"Can't. Too much work to do."

"You got to do chores with us," Cheryl said, staring at Amy.

For a split second, Amy thought the look in Hank's eyes turned crafty. "Yeah, it's a tradition on the ranch that every guest helps out with chores."

Was he kidding? She glanced at him again and his face was the picture of innocence.

Cheryl rested her head on Hank's shoulder, sent Amy a pleading look and said, "Please?"

She reached her arms toward Amy. Hank handed the child to her.

When Cheryl wrapped her arms around Amy's neck, Amy stiffened, then hugged the child. Such a sweet, trusting soul. How could Amy say no?

She nodded and followed Hank to the barn with Cheryl's warm weight resting against her chest.

She stopped just shy of the doors. "Are there cows in the barn?" Cows were big, ungraceful creatures Amy didn't hold any affection for.

"No, Amy. Horses." Hank stepped into the dark, cool interior. "When a structure houses horses we call it a stable, not a barn."

Amy crossed the threshold and halted. The two closest stalls had horses in them. *Really* big horses.

One of the horses stuck his head over the gate of his stall and let out a loud whinny. Amy jumped and Cheryl giggled.

Hank spun around to stare at Cheryl. He grinned. "You laughed," he said.

He took her from Amy and tossed her into the air.

"Don't—" Amy gasped, watching the child soar toward the ceiling, but Hank laughed and caught her easily, barely straining his muscles.

Cheryl smiled and stared into Hank's eyes in a union of souls that had Amy leaning forward, even as she wanted to run.

Hank set Cheryl on the floor and clapped his hands together. "Looks like the rest of the kids're done chores and are already outside. Sooner we get our share done, sooner we're off for fun and games."

The only game Amy wanted to play was called accounting.

Hank walked down the wide center aisle to the back and threw a door open. Sunlight flooded the far end of the stable.

"Can you open that second door at the front?" he called to Amy. "There's a hook on the outside wall to hold it open."

Amy did as he asked.

Hank carried pitchforks up the aisle. "Good. Fresh air." He tossed a tool to Amy. She barely caught it.

"You take that stall." He pointed to the one beside the huge horse on the right.

The horse hung his head over the gate. Amy put a wide berth between them when she entered the stall beside his.

Zeus was Hank's horse. No one else rode him. The horse could be temperamental or cooperative, depending on his mood. He could also be the best friend a man could ever hope to have in an animal.

Hank stared at the expensive sandals on Amy's feet, watched the woman enter the stall to muck it out and knew those shoes wouldn't last five minutes before they were toast.

"Wasteful," he whispered.

"Wait," he said out loud.

He rummaged through a cupboard at the back of the stable and came up with a pair of old boots. Cracks in the leather were crusted with manure. They smelled worse than the back end of a cow. As he carried them to Amy, his smile felt more than a little wicked.

"Here," he said. "You don't want to ruin those shoes. These belong to my ranch hand, Jenny. She's out with the campers. You'll meet her in a couple of days."

Amy took the boots and held them at arm's length, her perfect nose wrinkling in disgust.

"Relax," he said, "the smell grows on you."

With a grin that felt as wide as Montana, he walked to the stall he was about to muck out.

He kept an eye on her, though. No sense not enjoying the city slicker putting on a show.

Because she held the boots by the barest possible contact of fingertips to smelly leather, she had trouble pulling them on. When she tried to put on the second one, she fell back against the wall between her stall and Zeus's. She'd just recovered her footing when the stallion stuck his head over the wall and nudged her shoulder. She fell facedown into the straw and screamed.

Hank coughed to cover a laugh.

On hands and knees, she glared at him. He pretended a deep interest in his work.

"Is something funny?" she asked, her tone dangerously quiet.

He shook his head. "Naw. Just some dust in the air." He coughed again.

As she stood, Zeus trumpeted a laugh of his own. There were times when Hank suspected the horse was half human.

"Perceptive," Hank murmured.

He peered toward the open front door, where he'd set up a stool for Cheryl. She sat in the sun, weaving strips of leather, thinking—as Hank had led her to believe—that she was doing an important chore.

From the corner of his eye, Hank glimpsed Zeus dipping his head into his own stall.

Amy stood with her back to him, brushing straw from her knees, muttering furiously. Zeus's head reappeared over the dividing wall between the two stalls, a huge whack of straw dangling from his mouth.

Oh, no. Hank knew what was coming. He opened his mouth to warn Amy. Too late.

Zeus leaned forward and dumped the load onto Amy's head. She shrieked.

Hank laughed. He couldn't help it. He laughed until his sides hurt. He probably would have kept going except he heard Cheryl crying.

Hank hurried down the aisle and picked up Cheryl.

"Hush," he said. "It's only a joke. Amy isn't hurt."

Zeus neighed, shook his handsome head side to side, his glossy black mane flying, and pranced sideways.

Amy rounded on the horse. "You did that on purpose," she yelled. Then she turned on Hank. "Did you put him up to this?"

"Nope," he answered, laughter still tinting his voice. She was more fun than a barrel of rodeo clowns.

Amy put her hands on her hips and eyed Hank, suspicion written all over her face.

Cheryl placed a hand on Hank's cheek and

turned his head toward her. She looked into his eyes and said, "Don't hurt her."

Hank's heart constricted. Amy rushed over.

"It's okay, sweetheart." She patted Cheryl's back. "Hank is teasing me."

"That's right, darlin'," Hank said, but he wasn't looking at Cheryl. All of his attention was focused on the beautiful woman in front of him. "Amy is strong. She can take it."

Amy tilted her head to one side, her expression quizzical. "How do you know that?" she whispered.

"You must be, if you're here to face down your fears." He watched that one cheek turn red.

He could tell by her expression that he'd surprised her with his perception.

Lady, there are moments when your pain is written all over your face.

Hank took a couple of carrots from his shirt pocket.

"C'mere," he told Amy, stepping toward Zeus. "Watch this."

He handed the carrot to Cheryl. She held it out to Zeus, who took it from her hand like the mildest of lambs.

Hank gave a carrot to Amy. "A person can make friends with these creatures."

Amy grabbed the vegetable, thrust it toward Zeus, then leaped back the second the animal took it from her. Zeus ate the carrot, then thrust his nose toward Amy, nuzzling her neck. She jumped against Hank. He wrapped his free arm around her shoulders.

"That's nothing but a little affection from Zeus," he said.

With Cheryl sitting on one arm and a beautiful, warm woman nestled in the crook of the other, Hank felt a surge of longing. Holding a woman and a child like they were his own reminded him of his life before Jamie died and Macy left, before he lost his family.

He cleared his throat and stepped away from Amy. For darn sure, nothing was going to happen in that way with her.

AMY RETURNED to the house to wash up and don clean clothes. She stood in her room in bra and panties, scratching every inch she could reach. She pulled a piece of straw out of her bra.

A noise outside her open window drew her attention and she put on a robe. She crossed the room and looked out to the garden. Her eyes widened when she saw Hank outside with his hands cupped in front of him. His shirt and pants were dirty and wet, as though he'd been lying in mud and water.

A moment later, Amy discovered why. He squatted in front of the toad house, set down a toad, then placed the house on top of it.

Amy stretched her neck to watch as he snuck around the front corner of the house.

She heard the front door open.

"Hannah," Hank's voice called. "Where's Cheryl?"

"In here," Hannah answered. "In the kitchen."

Amy tiptoed to her bedroom door and opened it. The kitchen door opened and Hank stepped into the hallway.

He stood in front of her with Cheryl in his arms. He grinned at Amy—his eyes crinkled and his cheeks broadened, framing his white, white teeth—and something happened in her chest. A bubble rose from somewhere around her solar plexus.

Carrying Cheryl to the front door like she was a rare hothouse flower, Hank struggled to don his boots without using his hands.

"I got a surprise for you, darlin'," he said, smiling at the girl in his arms, then exiting the house. The bubble rose a little higher in Amy's chest.

She ran to her window and waited for them to round the corner, her heart pounding an odd skipping rhythm.

Hank set Cheryl on the ground in front of the toad house, then knelt beside her.

"Now crouch down here and I'll show you somethin'."

Cheryl's pip-squeak voice said, "'Kay." Then she mimicked his stance.

The bubble rose into Amy's throat. She had trouble swallowing around it.

Hank picked up the toad house. The toad hopped out. Cheryl screamed and jumped against Hank, grabbing him around the neck.

He laughed. "This little guy won't hurt you." He took Cheryl's hand in his own and brought it to the toad's back.

"He feels cool." Cheryl's voice shook, with fear or fascination—Amy wasn't sure which—but the child didn't pull her hand away. She kept it on the toad's back, tucked under Hank's big hand.

Amy thought she could almost feel that hand on her own, the surrounding safe warmth of it, the rough calluses, the dampness from the June heat.

Oh, my-y-y-y.

The bubble rising in her burst out of her mouth and she laughed. Hank looked up at the window.

He winked.

Oh, my.

She laughed again.

Amazing. When had she last laughed before coming to this ranch? She couldn't remember. Two years ago, she supposed. Then the memory of everything that had happened during that time resurrected and the bubble sank into the pit of her stomach.

Her hands shook. How could she go through with this? Start to like these people, when she'd cauterized and closed off her heart for more than two years? She wanted her joy in life back, but was terrified of getting close to people. Was one possible without the other?

She turned away from the window and got dressed. Needing to avoid Hank for a few hours, she wandered into the kitchen. "Hannah, could I eat lunch in here today?"

Hannah shook her head. "Sorry. I have to use the table for my pastry as soon as I give those kids their lunch."

"Okay." Amy gave in to the inevitable and walked into the hall in time to see Hank and Willie about to enter the dining room. The kids set up a noisy chatter at the table.

"They don't stand a chance in heaven of winning that game," Hank said to Willie.

"They're gonna win for sure." Willie scratched the back of his head.

"Want to bet?" Hank asked. Amy's stomach dropped. She wouldn't have taken Hank for a gambling man.

"How much?" Not Willie, too. She set her jaw.

"Twenty bucks."

"You're on." They shook hands and turned into the dining room.

Amy's antennae went on alert. The hairs on her arms stood up. She knew from experience what gambling could do. Was it possible Hank had an addiction that was costing him the ranch? It didn't seem likely—these kids meant too much—but the illness could spiral. She recalled the terrible fear she'd felt after her father died and left her and Mother with less than nothing, without even a roof over their heads.

She shivered. One little bet now and then wasn't an addiction, was it?

Surely Hank's bet on a sports game was innocent?

Wasn't it?

CHAPTER SIX

WHEN AMY HAD FINISHED lunch, she followed everyone out of the dining room, but stopped when Hannah called her.

The housekeeper approached with a portable phone clutched in her fist.

"It's for you."

"Me?" *Mother?* Who else would it be? Her stomach tightened. *What's happened?*

"Hello? Mother?"

"Is this Amy Graves?" a husky female voice asked.

"Yes. Who is this?"

"My name is Bernice Whitlow. I own the beauty salon in Ordinary."

Amy collapsed onto a chair. Mother wasn't hurt. "How can I help you?" she asked. Was this a sales call? Did Bernice want to show the big-city girl what she could do in her salon?

"I've got a woman sitting in my shop," Bernice answered, "who says she's your mother."

"What?"

"She just got off the bus. It stops right outside my door. She looked pale, so I invited her into my shop."

"Let me speak to her. Please."

A brief minute later, Amy's mother said, "Hello, dear."

"Mother, what on earth are you doing in Ordinary?"

"I came to visit you, sweetheart. Isn't that nice?"

Amy gritted her teeth. Mother could have gotten lost, or gotten on the wrong bus, or ended up in Timbuktu.

"Don't move." Amy's voice sounded harsh and she tried to modulate it. "I'll be there in half an hour."

Amy set the phone on the hall table.

Before she picked up her mother, she had to ask Hank whether he would mind another guest.

It took her awhile to hunt him down. She finally found him across a long field, crouching in the grass with the children and naming wildflowers for them.

"Hank, can I have a word with you?" She gestured away from the children.

He nodded and followed her twenty or so feet away, where she glanced around. A brilliant gem of a sun sat in the wide blue sky and warmed Hank's fields.

"Do you ever grow tired of this magnificent view?" Amy asked.

When he didn't answer, she turned to him. He watched her with raised eyebrows.

"What?" she asked.

"That's the first nice thing you've said about the ranch since you got here."

Was she really so self-involved? "It's a lovely ranch."

"Thanks."

"Well?" she asked. "Do you ever tire of this?"

"Naw." He smiled. "Haven't yet, and that's thirty-seven years and counting. Don't think I ever will."

"Hank, I wonder if you might have another bedroom available? It doesn't have to be large. A small one would be fine."

"You don't like your room?"

"Yes, I like it." She crossed her arms and gathered her courage. "It wouldn't be for me. It would be for my mother. I received a call from a woman in town named Bernice."

"Bernice Whitlow? What did she want?"

"My mother just got off a bus in Ordinary. I didn't invite her," she said, worried he would think she would presume so much. "She won't be any trouble. I promise. I'll take care of her."

A slow smile lit Hank's face. "Sure, bring her here. I'd like to meet her."

Just like that, he would let her stay? That easily? Perhaps he didn't understand the significance of what Amy was saying. "She would have to stay as long as I do. And she'd need a ground floor room—she doesn't do stairs as well as she once did."

"Your mother is welcome here. And if you don't mind moving, she could have the room you're using."

Amy shook her head, bemused. What a generous man.

"I'd better run. She's waiting for me."

"Take your time," Hank said. "Your mother is in good hands with Bernice."

The town of Ordinary was like something from a bygone era. Max Wright's Grocery Store had displays of produce outside without personnel guarding the stock. A sign on the window advertised Free Delivery. She hadn't seen a sign like that in the city since she was a kid.

Beside the grocery store, bright-red geraniums ran the length of the sill in the window of Bernice's Beauty Salon.

The salon cozied up next to Scotty's Hardware. Stores with straightforward names. Owner proud, Amy guessed, and smiled.

A middle-aged man she assumed was Scotty swept the sidewalk in front of the hardware store and waved as she stepped out of her car.

"Met Gladys, Amy," he called. "Real nice lady."

Wow. He knew her name and her mother's name. Friendly interest, or was this a fishbowl community?

A bell tinkled when Amy opened the door of the salon. A middle-aged, buxom blonde turned as Amy entered.

"Hi, honey. I'm Bernice." She held out her hand and smiled warmly. "Your mother's fine. We've been having a cozy chat."

Amy shook her hand and whispered, "Thank you." How could a stranger be so friendly? "You saw my mother outside?"

"Mm-hmm. She looked hot, like she needed to sit down in a cool spot for a while."

"So you just asked her in?"

Bernice looked surprised by the question. "Of course. Poor dear. She didn't look well. C'mon. She's in the back."

She led Amy to a spit-shined, tidy back room, where she found Mother sitting on a small pink damask sofa reading a magazine, a colorful afghan across her lap, a cup of tea on a small table beside her. Right at home.

"Mother?"

Mother looked up, as sweetly surprised to see Amy as if she hadn't spoken to her on the phone half an hour ago.

"Amy, how wonderful to see you."

Amy didn't smile. "Mother, what possessed

you to come here on the bus alone?" Her voice was sharp with worry. "Any number of things could have happened to you."

Her mother patted her hand. "But they didn't, dear, did they?"

She held up the magazine that rested on her lap. "Look. Brad and Angelina are fighting again. Why can't those movie stars ever be nice to each other?"

Amy smiled reluctantly. She never could stay angry at Mother for long.

"Are you ready to go?" she asked. "We shouldn't impose on Bernice any longer."

Mother rose, folded the afghan, then laid it across the back of the sofa. She followed Amy to the front of the shop.

Amy turned to Bernice. "Thank you so much." A flush of gratitude overwhelmed her. She shuddered at the thought of Mother getting off a bus in a strange town without help.

Bernice waved her hand. "Anyone else in town would have done the same for her, you know."

Amy didn't know. She didn't know this town well enough to trust everyone.

Just before they stepped through the open doorway, Bernice engulfed Mother in a warm hug.

"Lovely to meet you, Gladys. You c'mon in for those highlights we talked about. My treat."

"Thank you, Bernice." Mother followed Amy outside. "Isn't she a dear?"

"Yes, she is," Amy answered, bemused. "It was good of her to take you in."

About to launch into her lecture about the dangers of traveling alone for senior citizens, Amy caught herself, arrested by the look on Mother's face. Avid curiosity. She swung her head from side to side, taking in as much as she could about Ordinary. She drank in every detail of small-town life.

Amy noticed the candy shop across the street with a sign that read Sweet Talk and remembered Hank's humbugs.

She made an impulsive decision. "Mother, do you remember how much we used to like humbugs?"

"Yes. They were wonderful, weren't they?"

"That shop has a sign in the window that says they have old-fashioned candies. I'm going to check it out."

Amy opened the passenger door of her Audi and settled Mother in out of the sun. "I'm going to run over. I'll be right back."

As she entered the shop, the man behind the counter greeted her. "What can I get for you?" His smile spoke volumes about how attractive he found her.

She glanced around at the shop's rich styling—dark wood-paneled walls, white porcelain counters and green and rose stained-glass lamps hanging above, swaying slightly from brass chains.

"This place is fabulous," she murmured.

She picked up a couple of pounds of assorted candies she hadn't seen in ages—SweeTarts, Candy Buttons, Licorice Pipes, Pixy Stix, Mike & Ikes, Marshmallow Cones—as a gift for the ranch. Probably not too smart bringing a bunch of candy to kids but, she thought defiantly, those kids deserved treats.

"Do you carry humbugs?"

"Sure do. How much do you want?"

She picked up a pound of humbugs and thanked him profusely for his service.

"My name's Colin John Wright," the man said. "Most everyone calls me C.J." He smiled. So sweet.

She smiled, said goodbye and stepped out of the shop.

A cow ambled by. On the road. On the main street of Ordinary. Strange.

"Did you see that, Amy?" Mother asked as Amy climbed in the car. "It was a cow."

"Yep, I saw it." She tossed the bag of candy into Mother's lap, then gunned the engine.

Mother handed her a humbug as Amy pulled a neat U-turn on Main Street and headed out of town. The flavor of mint burst on Amy's tongue.

"I like it here," Mother said.

Amy rolled down her window and slowed the car to study the town. Now that her mother was safe beside her, she had the time to give in to curiosity. Small towns had always seemed so foreign to her.

Ordinary, Montana, possessed more charm than Amy had expected.

Tall, black lamps with glass heads, imitating old-fashioned gas lamps, lined both sides of the street. Hung from brackets mounted high on each post, peat-lined wire pots overflowed with pink ivy geraniums and white alyssum.

The New America Diner caught her eye. It advertised an all-day breakfast—bacon, eggs, toast and "the best home fries this side of Butte" for $4.99. The New America must have been "new" way back in the fifties, but now showed its age in an old sign and flaking paint. Every table in the window was full, though. That said all a person needed to know about the place.

The scent of roast beef drifted on the tame breeze.

A tall, handsome man stepped out of the diner and nestled a cowboy hat onto his dark hair. He was herding two small children. A woman wearing jeans, a plaid shirt and red cowboy boots followed. They looked happy.

Amy couldn't really remember what happy felt like.

Two boys scooted by on bicycles. "Turn right,"

the second boy yelled to the one at the front. "Let's go to the park."

On the other side of the diner stood the police station, then a store called The Price is Right, boasting gently used clothing.

A sign on a pretty shop caught her eye. To Boldly Grow.

Amy laughed. A *Star Trek* fan, just like herself. She'd have to meet the florist one day. Amy had gotten hooked on reruns of the original series. She loved the sci-fi corniness of it and had become a Trekkie, but only in secret. Tony had been disgusted with her, said it was unsophisticated, dumb. Told her not to tell his friends.

With a shrug, Amy thought, *I don't care what you think anymore, Tony.*

Time to become proud of her own idiosyncrasies.

The Stars and Stripes hanging above the door of the post office waved in a gentle breeze.

"Simply lovely." Mother sighed.

"Yes, it is," Amy murmured.

She glanced at the expanse of green and brown fields under the huge Montana sky as they drove toward the ranch. She breathed deeply of young sprouting grasses and dark earth.

Mother caught her breath. "Oh, Amy, it's so beautiful, isn't it?"

Amy nodded, captivated by a landscape that had felt foreign to her only yesterday.

They arrived at the ranch and Amy came around the car to open Mother's door and help her out.

Mother stood and took in the landscape and the weeping willow on the lawn and the white house with the blue shutters.

"Oh, what a pretty place." She sighed.

Hank came out of the house and walked toward them, a soft smile splitting his face as he stared at her mother. Amy tried to see her as he would.

She looked almost perky, wearing her favorite dress—the navy-blue-and-white polka-dotted, short-sleeved one Amy had given her for Christmas two years ago.

Her hair was a perfectly groomed, sleek little cap of gray with strands of auburn running through it—few and far between these days. An older version of Amy's own green eyes watched Hank. Wrinkles creased the corners of her eyes and mouth, deeper than Amy remembered them being. Even so, Mother was aging gracefully. She was a lovely sixty-five-year-old.

Hank approached and extended his hand. "Hello. You must be Amy's mother. I would have recognized you anywhere. I see she got her beauty from you."

Amy nearly rolled her eyes before she realized he wasn't laying on phony flattery. He was serious and Mother blushed.

"Mother, this is Hank Shelter." Amy rested her hand on her mother's shoulder. "Hank, my mother, Gladys Graves."

Hank took the hand he held and placed it on his forearm. "Pleased to meet you, Mrs. Graves."

"Call me Gladys. It doesn't sound as old, does it?"

Hank smiled at her. "We've got a room ready for you."

"You have?"

"Yes. It looks out over that flower garden."

"I love flowers, don't I, Amy?" She didn't wait for her daughter's response, Amy noticed, she was so taken by the big cowboy giving her his undivided attention.

Hank drew Gladys under the shade of the tree, where they talked quietly like old friends, leaving Amy to get Mother's one bag out of the trunk.

Later, Amy settled herself in the room tucked under the eaves in the attic, three flights up. Hank carried her suitcase upstairs and set it on the homemade patchwork quilt covering the bed. When he stood up, he banged his head on the low, slanted ceiling.

"I hope this room works out for you," he said, removing his cowboy hat and punching the dent out of it. "You know, I thought your mother would be a lot younger than she is."

Amy crossed the room—three short steps—to

the window to open it. She couldn't breathe. The room was too small, no larger than her childhood room in Butte. How was she going to sleep in here, with the dark-stained wooden ceiling bearing down on her like a weight?

At least the walls were dry. No water stains on musty wallpaper—unlike that long-ago room. This room smelled like dry cedar.

Finally answering Hank, she said, "Most people assume that my mother will be younger than she is. I was a relatively late child."

"Me, too," Hank said.

Amy stared out at the view. At least there was plenty of space outside. Hank's land seemed to go on forever.

She looked over her shoulder at him. "I've wondered why there's such a big age difference between you and Leila."

"Leila and I had different mothers. Her mother died when she was little. Dad married his second wife, my mom, years later. Leila was fifteen when I was born. My mother died years ago."

"I'm sorry," Amy mumbled. Her mother was a burden at times, but Amy couldn't imagine life without her. "So that's why you and Leila are so different?"

"Yup. As different as night and day. She takes after Dad." He cleared his throat. "Sorry this room isn't much."

"It's fine." She paced to the bed—three short steps from the window.

Hank blushed. "Naw, it isn't big enough. We're full to the rafters right now. You can move to the second floor once this set of kids leaves." Hank stood inside the door with his hands in his pockets.

"When is that?" she asked.

"At the end of this week."

So many children came through here. How could he stand to say goodbye so often?

"That's a shorter visit than I would have thought," she said.

"They got here two weeks before you did. They stay for three weeks, leaving us one week out of each month to pull the ranch back together and get ready for the next set."

Hank leaned his big shoulder against the doorjamb, filling the doorway, making the room feel about as small as the nearly nonexistent closet. He smelled lemony and a touch spicy. Tangy. So unlike the thick aftershave Tony used.

Even three feet away, Amy felt heat radiating from his big body. She sure wouldn't need many blankets if she slept with him.

She pulled up short at that thought. If she *slept* with him? Where on earth had that come from?

Standing abruptly, she opened her suitcase. "This room will be just fine," she told Hank in her best take-charge tone, fooling him even if she couldn't fool herself. He left the room.

After unpacking, she returned to the first floor and went in to dinner. Mother was already there with everyone else, sitting at the other end of the table on Hank's right. They talked quietly throughout the meal. Mother lapped up the attention like a flower starved for moisture.

A frisson of guilt fluttered through Amy's stomach. She should have given Mother more of her time in Billings. What kind of daughter was she?

THE FOLLOWING MORNING, after settling Mother in the living room with tea and magazines, Amy went in search of Hank.

"I need to get into that office," she said when she spotted him near the open front door.

He pretended he didn't hear her and turned to leave, but Amy knew there was *no way* he hadn't heard her. She ran across the foyer and shut the door before he could leave.

She squeezed between him and the closed door and said, "Where is the key?" She wasn't taking no for an answer today.

He stepped back. "I lost it?"

She shook her head and laughed. "Uh-uh. That lie smells as bad as the pile of manure behind the stables."

He reached into his pocket. Amy wondered why he looked wary. What on earth was in that office?

HANK OPENED the office door and allowed Amy to step inside ahead of him.

He tried to see the room from a visitor's perspective.

Rodeo belt buckles, tidy and free of dust, lined a shelf along one wall. A profusion of photos in matching frames covered the walls above the shelves in marching order.

Hundreds of unframed snapshots of children in small white cowboy hats papered another wall, his favorite part of the house.

Two overstuffed burgundy leather armchairs, one on either side of his massive desk, and bookshelves lining two walls filled the floor space.

Hank shied away from looking at the papers that littered the desk.

Amy wandered closer to the photographs above the belt buckles.

In one, Hank sat on a rearing horse, holding on to the reins with one hand.

Another showed the same pose, but on a bull who had his hind legs in the air and his massive head and chest near the ground, straining with all his might to unseat his rider, while Hank sat erect on the bull's back.

"Dear God!" Amy exclaimed, and pointed to one of the photos. "That bull's head is three times the size of yours."

"Yeah," he said. "They are big animals."

She pointed to a photo of a bull chasing a clown. The bull, Razorblade, had tried to gore Hank's backside a split second after he'd jumped over a fence. Razorblade's horns had taken a sizable chunk out of the wood.

"That was the last time I volunteered to be a clown," Hank said, smiling. "Won't do it again anytime soon. Most dangerous job in the rodeo."

Amy stared at Hank, looked him up and down.

"How tall are you?" she asked.

"Six-two." What did that have to do with anything?

She nodded toward the photo. "You're a big man, you've got wide shoulders, great biceps, but you're dwarfed by that bull."

She looked angry, but he was too caught up in her comment on his biceps to worry.

"What on earth possessed you to do something so foolish?" she asked in a harsh voice. "Cowboys are every bit as mortal as anyone else on earth."

Hank bristled. "The regular guy was sick. You have to have a clown to distract the bull once he's tossed his rider, to give the guy a chance to get out of the way."

She shivered. "But *why* would a person get on a bull in the first place?"

Hank bit the inside of his cheek, then said, "I guess you have to be raised in the culture to understand it."

Amy frowned and stepped away. "You're right. My apologies. Rule number one in business, don't criticize the client's work."

He heard the unspoken end of the sentence, "Or his hobby or whatever the rodeo is to him." Her calling him a client rankled. Reminded him she was here to work.

She gestured toward the chaos on top of the desk. It looked like every paper that had ever entered this house was stacked there.

Hank hated like hell for her to see the paperwork that way, but he'd never figured out how to deal with it. Willie was no help. He couldn't file, either.

"Tell me what's what here," Amy said. "Where are your ledgers?"

Hank cleared his throat. "My what?"

"The ledgers," Amy repeated.

Hank couldn't breathe, knew that his face looked blank. He didn't have a clue what she was talking about.

"Your financial statements?" she asked.

He gestured toward the piles scattered around the room. "You'll find everything to do with the ranch here. Any of the older stuff my dad took care of will be in the drawers or in there." He pointed to a short filing cabinet tucked into a corner behind the door.

Amy frowned at the confusion. "But the rest of the ranch is so neat."

The tips of Hank's ears felt hot. Man, he hated this. Yeah, he was good at lots of other things, but not paperwork, or office stuff.

He needed to get out of here and spun around to head into the hall.

"But—" He heard her speak as he hit the hallway racing. He set his feet in the direction of the door. If he hurried, he might get out of here before she managed to catch him and complain about his methods. She'd have every right. The screen door slammed shut behind him when he left the house.

She stayed in that office for hours. She'd only been here for two days, but today Hank missed her in his truck and in the stable doing chores. At the start, he'd had plans to get her off his ranch as soon as possible. Yet now, irrationally, he wanted her around longer.

He wanted her to spend time with him, not to uncover things that were better left hidden.

She made him feel his own faults too keenly, but she also made him long for things he hadn't thought about in years. Sharing, teaching new things, holding, kissing.

He needed to show her more of his land, to make her proud of him and the work he did with the kids.

She was a smart lady. She'd have her work done by the end of the week if he didn't slow her down in some way. And inspiration for that came the moment he spotted Cheryl.

"You like Amy, don't you?" he asked the little girl.

Cheryl nodded.

"Do you want to spend time with her in the office?"

Cheryl nodded again.

"Okay, you can do that. Just knock on the door."

Using Cheryl to keep Amy away from all of that paperwork was low, but a man did what a man had to do in this life.

A TIMID KNOCK on the closed office door pulled Amy away from her task. She straightened and rubbed the small of her back.

"Come in."

The door opened slowly, then Cheryl stepped into the room.

"Yes?" Amy asked.

The child stared at her with wide dark eyes. "What are you doing?"

"Work. I'm busy," Amy blurted, unnerved by the wisdom in those eyes—a child old before her time.

Cheryl approached the desk and patted Amy's lap. "Can I sit here?"

"I—" Amy tried to say no but couldn't. Cheryl had already wiggled her way under Amy's skin. She nodded.

Cheryl climbed onto her lap. "Can I work, too?"

Amy placed a timid kiss on Cheryl's head. She handed her a sheet of paper and a pencil, then started shuffling piles of envelopes and receipts around on the desk, trying to concentrate on work again. But all she could think about was Cheryl's weight on her legs and the warm breath that whispered through the child's open mouth onto Amy's hand.

Amy felt her throat clog. The skin on the back of Cheryl's neck looked as pale as a newborn chick's. Amy ran one finger down her nape and found it unbearably soft.

A ragged sigh escaped Amy as she set her hand on the girl's shoulder. Tenderness welled in her. She gave in to the inevitable. The child was capturing her heart.

HOURS AFTER he'd sent Cheryl in, Hank stood in front of the closed office door, *his* office door, hesitating to face that woman again. He came out on the short end whenever he talked to her. Remembering her asking why anyone would get on an angry bull, he felt a lump form in his throat. She'd meant, who would be that stupid? Sometimes he'd wondered that himself. Well, she'd sure pegged him, hadn't she?

But what about all the others involved in the rodeo? They had more than a few useless screws rattling around their brains. He knew for a fact they weren't all stupid.

He cracked the knuckles of his right hand, then the left. He had to find a way to make her like him and his ranch.

"You gonna stand there all night?"

Hank whirled to find Hannah's elfin face peeking around the kitchen door.

"Supper is getting cold," she said. "Amy will be hungry. Cheryl, too."

As quickly as she had appeared, Hannah was gone. Hank heard the clatter of plates as she set the dining room table.

Taking a deep breath, he knocked.

"Yes?" came the muffled response. Even through the thick oak door, she had a beautiful voice.

"Melodious," he whispered. He'd always wanted to use that word.

The door opened in front of him and there she stood, pretty, flawless and unwrinkled. He felt dirty from the football game with the kids. He'd only had time to wash his hands and splash water on his face.

He hadn't even combed his hair. He flattened it against his head with both hands, trying to tame it.

"Mangy." He'd always wanted to use that word, too.

"I beg your pardon?" A frown creased Amy's forehead.

"Nothing." He smiled thinly. "I was just wondering if you wanted to join us for dinner."

AMY TOOK HER CHAIR at the table beside Willie. Mother sat on Hank's right. Hank chose what looked like the biggest piece of chicken on the platter and placed it on Mother's plate. They smiled at each other.

Amy felt a twinge of envy that they were developing a bond already, while all she seemed to do was aggravate the man in one way or another. But sometimes, the way he looked at her made her feel...good, itchy, very, very female.

Mother laughed and Amy felt that flicker of envy again.

Oh, get over yourself, and let Mother enjoy her visit here. Even with the reprimand, Amy's attention rarely left the opposite end of the table and the meal stretched on.

Afterward, Amy retreated to the office. She stared at the photos of the many children on the wall, the ones Hank had brought here after his son died. Was one of these kids Jamie? Hank must have started his family so young, when he was barely out of high school. Was that how they did things in rural communities?

Did she really want to know which one was Jamie? It would only sadden her to look at his tiny face and know that Hank would never see his son again. As she always did, she took refuge in her work. Time to update the client. She picked up her cell phone and phoned Leila.

When she answered, Amy asked, "Are you still in Seattle?"

"Yes. I'll be here a few more days. How's the ranch?"

"It's lovely here."

"What did you find out?"

Amy heard the concern in Leila's voice. "I have nothing to tell you yet. Just wanted to let you know what I'm up against here." She eyed the stacks of papers on the desk. "You should see the mess I started to wade through this afternoon. This is the most disorganized set of finances I've ever seen. All I've had time to do is houseclean."

She didn't mention that she'd been slowed by the sweetest little girl and had enjoyed every minute of it.

More papers lay scattered on the floor, where they'd fallen when she'd tried to sort them.

"I don't understand it." Leila's strong voice sounded like it came from the room next door rather than miles away. "Dad only died a year ago. He would have kept everything up. He was an organized man."

"Was he suffering from Alzheimer's?"

"The man was smart as a whip until the day he died. I'm sure he would have taught Hank his filing system. Hank isn't a lazy man."

"Hmm. Well, when I have news for you, I'll call."

"Maybe you should visit the bank. According to their letter, they want to foreclose unless that mortgage is paid. Why on earth isn't Hank paying it?"

"I can't help you yet, Leila, until I sort through all of the paperwork. I don't know where the money is going if not against that mortgage."

Amy lowered her voice. "You do know that if things are as bad as the bank says, you will need to sell the ranch. Immediately. Before the bank has the chance to foreclose and you lose everything."

"I'll take your expert advice on that," Leila answered. "We'll do whatever you think best."

How uncharacteristic of Leila to give me control, Amy thought as she hung up, but had no time to mull it over. Hank stood in the doorway, his lips pinched in a thin line. Oh, dear. He'd heard what she'd said. Why hadn't she closed the door?

"Who are you?" he asked, his voice tight.

She frowned. "What do you mean?"

"Why does Leila trust you so much? She isn't like that with anyone."

"Leila and I met five years ago, when she took aerobics classes I was teaching. We hit it off." She raised one shoulder, then dropped it. "I'm not sure why. She's a couple of decades older than me and we have such different personalities, but our affection for each other is real."

The hard edges of Hank's face eased a bit.

"Leila helped me through some difficult years," Amy said. "I owe her my help."

Hank looked resigned and turned to leave. Amy stopped him. Might as well get everything out into the open.

"You'll have to face the truth at some point, Hank," she said. "Selling might be your only alternative."

He turned back. "There is nothing wrong with the money and the ranch," he insisted.

"The letter from the bank says something completely different. They're talking about foreclosure."

Hank's eyes widened and his jaw dropped. He took a step into the office. "Foreclosure? That's impossible. The bank told me everything is fine."

Amy frowned. What on earth was going on?

Hank's hands clenched and unclenched at his sides.

"Leila would go along with selling the ranch?"

"Yes," Amy said. "I believe she would."

"Why did Dad give the ranch to her? Why didn't he will it to both of us?"

Amy shook her head, regretful that she couldn't help him out. She had no idea what the family dynamics were.

"Why can't *you* do something to fix this?" he asked.

"I'll do everything I can, but if you've mismanaged your funds, then you will have to pay the consequences."

Hank stared at her as if she was something disgusting. It hurt, coming from a man she knew to be kind. She was not the villain here. Why couldn't he see that?

She opened her mouth to say as much, but Hank stalked away, slamming the door behind him as he left the house.

CHAPTER SEVEN

AT BEDTIME, Amy went searching for Mother to tell her good-night.

She found her bedroom empty. She peeked into the bathroom across the hall. Empty.

Where on earth was she?

Then she heard the faint sound of voices in the living room. Checking across the hall, she found that room empty, but the TV in the rec room cast a blue glow on that end of the room. Amy walked around the double-sided fireplace.

Hank and Mother sat on the small chintz love seat in front of the TV. Alex Trebek was introducing the contestants of that night's game of *Jeopardy!* Hank must have taped it earlier. The fact that he already knew that Gladys loved the show and provided her access to it said so much about his character.

Something melted in her, that this big guy would do that for Mother, a woman he barely knew.

"Let's get started, shall we? Keith, you first." Alex Trebek's cultured voice directed the game.

Amy stayed out of sight, peeking around the huge fireplace to watch.

A young man with a clear baby-faced complexion chose the first category. "Famous women for two hundred."

In the show's trademark tradition, Alex read the answer, "In 1900, she persuaded the University of Rochester to admit women."

Keith asked the question, "Who was Susan B. Anthony?" At the exact same moment, Gladys and Hank asked the same thing, startling Amy.

"Right for two hundred dollars," Alex said. "Keith, your turn again."

"Musical instruments. Two hundred."

"This is closely related to the virginal, but is strung diagonally, and is generally wing-shaped rather than square."

"What is a spinet?" Hank asked in a split second. Amy felt her jaw drop. How did Hank know that?

She listened for another ten minutes. Hank got every answer right, with Mother coming a close second.

A commercial came on, louder than the show. Hank hit the mute button.

"Smart kid," he said about the contestant in the lead.

"So are you," Mother said.

"You think so?" Hank answered, the wonderful

smile beneath his dark mustache warm enough to melt butter. "You're not so bad yourself."

Amy stared at the back of Gladys's graying head, imagining that Mother's answering smile was just as warm. The sigh Amy smothered felt wistful. She wanted that intimacy between herself and Hank and, yet, the idea of getting close to him—to any man—was inconceivable. The thought of exposing her scarred body terrified her.

She left the room without a sound.

"Well, what did you expect?" she whispered as she trudged up the stairs. She'd known since her fourteenth birthday that the world was an unfair and cruel place.

"Hey, it's better than being dead." She pressed a hand against the ache in her chest, remembering the time when she'd thought that maybe death was a good choice.

"Oh, stop it. Stop feeling sorry for yourself." In her bedroom, she threw her blouse from the bed onto the floor, then slid between the sheets.

She had enough on her plate these days without being jealous of her own mother.

ON THURSDAY MORNING, Amy found an old computer in the corner behind the filing cabinet.

She couldn't bring herself to ask Hank for his password. People were surprisingly predictable, though, in what they chose. By the time she decided on Sheltering Arms, she was surprised to find that it was wrong. She tried to recall whether Leila had ever mentioned her parents' names.

Then Amy remembered that the ranch used to be called the Lucky S. She typed it in. Eureka. Rubbing her hands together, she opened the business software.

An hour later, she felt like tearing her hair out. Nothing. Nada. Zip. All of the information stored on it was at least a year old. It must have been Hank's father's computer, not his.

She'd studied his records and, granted, they'd been extremely low on funds at the time, but they'd been scraping by, nowhere near foreclosure.

So whatever the problem was, it was Hank's. What was he doing wrong?

Maybe there was something in the stack of bank statements she'd so laboriously separated from the other papers. They began where the computer files ended—a little over a year ago.

Odd. Not one of the bank statements held a record of checks being written or bills being paid.

She studied the statements and a pattern emerged. A terrible realization formed. She'd seen this once before. Huge sums withdrawn to nowhere. Enormous sums. Disappearing. Regularly. Once a week. Sometimes more often. Last time she'd seen this problem, the company owner had been a gambler.

She remembered how hard Hank had tried to keep her out of the office.

She'd heard Hank tell Willie they'd have to sell one of the ranch's pickup trucks for much-needed cash.

She stared at piles of utility bills that hadn't been opened, let alone paid. How he still had electricity and telephone service was beyond her. She needed to get at those bills.

She'd found one huge credit card bill for hats—dozens of white Stetsons. Where were the hats, and why hadn't Hank paid the bill? Why wasn't there another letter hounding Hank for payment?

Though she had too many unanswered questions, she couldn't ignore the behavior. And it confirmed her earlier concern about Hank being a gambler.

Now she understood the whispering between Hank and Willie. "Ya gotta tell her!" she'd heard Willie whisper a couple of times.

She jumped up from the desk chair.

It couldn't be.

Not Hank.

Amy couldn't believe that Hank would treat his money so cavalierly, would take such huge chances with the livelihood that supported the kids for whom he had such a passion.

She also knew, though, that there were some impulses—addictions—people couldn't control.

Could Hank Shelter, that big, caring man, really be a gambler? She couldn't believe it, but the evidence was there in black and white.

She raced across the yard to the stable, stopping when she stood a foot away from Hank. The children were at the far end of the stable. Out of earshot.

"Why didn't you tell me?" she asked, her voice low.

His mouth went slack and his skin paled as his gaze slid from hers to the ground.

Oh, Hank. The weight of disappointment landed in Amy's stomach.

"Did you think you could hide your problem from me forever?" she asked.

He hung his head and shook it once.

She stepped close. "Gambling is a serious problem."

His head came up and he stared at her like a fish dying for air.

"Surprised I found out so quickly? You didn't do much to hide it."

"Can—" He cleared his throat. "Can you fix it?"

"I don't know," she said. "I'll try. But you lost a lot of money."

He surprised her. Where were his excuses? His

denials? Where were the empty promises of turning his luck around? People with addictions always had plenty to say in their own defense.

He stared past her to the light shining through the stable doors. In the dark interior, she watched Hank's jaw harden, saw his teeth clench.

"Save it," he ordered.

"What?"

"I said save it." The man was furious. Because she'd found out? Or because he hated his own weakness? "Save the ranch. Don't sell."

Sudden, irrational anger spurted through her. He wanted *her* to fix a huge problem of his own making? "I'll try, Hank," she said, her voice hard and loud, "but I'm not a miracle worker."

As she left the stables, she had enough awareness of her surroundings to remember those children at the far end of the building. *Oh please, don't have heard anything*. What was wrong with her? She never reacted this way in her work life.

Why was she so emotional with Hank? She'd behaved like a professional the last time she'd found this problem with a client. Why the difference today?

The answer came in a flash. She cared for Hank. Already. It was more than an attraction to his big cowboy body, and his magnetic smile. It was his love of the children, and his still-youthful spirit and enthusiasm, and the indomitable backbone that had him starting this program for children after his son's death. He could just as easily have faded away into grief, then mediocrity. But not Hank.

Get yourself under control. This is no way for a businesswoman to behave. You can limit what you feel for these people.

She had to stop her sentimentality from clouding her judgment and behavior before she proved herself unfit to do the job.

WHEN AMY ENTERED the living room before dinner, both the adults and children turned. They stared at her with an odd curiosity and a touch of resentment.

Amy's heart sank. They'd seen that she'd been angry with their friend, Hank.

He refused to meet her eye.

"Hello, sweetheart," Mother said from an armchair by the fireplace. Cheryl sat in her lap, looking at a book.

"Hi," Amy answered. Not a single smile in the roomful of people.

She wanted to yell, "I'm not the enemy. Hank screwed up, not me." The urge to point at Hank accusingly was so strong Amy curled her hands into fists.

Mother looked around the room then back to Amy with a frown.

It's not my fault.

She returned to the cubbyhole of the office, closing the door behind her to shut them all out. The room seemed to shrink around her. Amy turned on the desk lamp but it felt too bright and harsh, so she flicked the switch off.

HANK'S HEART felt like it would beat right out of his chest to lie bleeding on the carpet, in front of everyone.

He had a choice. He could let Amy continue to believe he was a gambler, or he could explain everything.

Willie sat beside him and whispered, "Ya gotta tell her the truth, Hank."

"Nope. Can't." If he thought the pain was bad now, it was nothing compared to what he would feel if Amy found out his real problem. A smart woman like her would think him the stupidest man on the planet.

Stupidest. Was that a real word?

"Hank," Willie said, "you gotta be the most stubborn person I know."

"Me?" Hank asked. "I'm a nice guy. Easygoing. Everyone says so."

"Yeah, easygoing everywhere in your life but one place."

Who could blame him? It was the one part of his character he truly hated. Most of the time he could forget that it even existed—then, unexpectedly, the truth would rear its ugly head again.

Hank couldn't read.

How could he possibly describe to Willie the depth of his shame? How could he explain that in this century a man his age couldn't read, hadn't been able to learn? Amy was so smart and he was so stupid.

He wouldn't risk telling her what was really wrong with him, but he was so damn tired of carrying the weight of his secret.

AMY SAT in the twilight of the office, frozen by indecision. What was her next step? She didn't want to face the ranch's finances again today. Yet she had a job to do. She needed all of her take-charge energy back. She needed it badly.

A quiet knock sounded and Mother stepped into the room, shutting the door behind her.

"What have you done?" she asked, an uncharacteristic sharpness in her tone.

"Why do you think I've done something?"

"Why is everyone giving you funny looks?"

"*I* haven't done anything." Pushing the chair out from the other side of the desk, Amy gestured for Mother to sit. "I'm trying to straighten out the finances here. The ranch has been losing money hand over fist."

She hesitated to tell Mother about Hank's

gambling. She didn't want to skew Mother's opinion of him, even if he did deserve it.

"Money has been pouring out of the ranch's bank accounts regularly for a year and I can't find where it's going."

"Yes, but why is everyone mad at you?"

The laugh Amy couldn't hold back sounded bitter. "It's part of the territory, Mother. Part of walking into companies to tell them how to run their businesses. Nobody wants to look at their mistakes, and heaven forbid you should ask them to change the way they do things."

"But the children...what do they have to do with the finances?"

"I think they know I was angry with Hank for a few minutes today." She sighed. "They worship him like a hero."

"He is their hero, Amy."

"I know, and he should be. The work he does here is amazing." She pushed her hair back from her face. "The children were at the far end of the stable and I didn't realize they'd heard me raise my voice with Hank."

"What about?"

"Mother—" Could she bring up Dad's problem with money after all these years? Did she really want to raise the specter of issues that should have died long ago? She stood behind the desk, leaning her damp palms on the cool, polished wood. "Mother, what was it like living with a man who didn't have any common sense where money was concerned? Who—who gambled it all away?"

"Hard." Mother didn't look surprised by the question. Perhaps she'd been waiting for Amy to finally ask about it.

Mother sat back, dwarfed by the leather armchair. With her hands resting peacefully in her lap, she resembled a small, white-haired, female Buddha. "But I loved him. I never stopped loving him."

"Even after he died and left us with nothing but debts?"

"Even then. I was terrified without him, but I still loved him. He was a weak man in that one way, but good in so many others." She stared out the window and her gaze became unfocused. "He was generous, would give a person the last nickel in his pocket. Do you remember how he sent you to the store every night for a box of Cracker Jack popcorn? You used to love it."

Amy's throat hurt. "I remember. All the good stuff seemed to get lost after his death, though."

Amy lowered her head away from the compassion on Mother's face and the understanding in her eyes. She straightened an already perfectly aligned pile of paper.

"Why these questions about your father?"

Amy shrugged.

"Why tonight?" Mother persisted. "What happened?"

Amy huffed out a breath of air but said nothing.

"What does it have to do with the ranch?" Mother asked, her voice stronger than Amy had heard it in years. "Answer me."

Amy had to tell someone, to share this astounding news. "It's Hank. He's been robbing the ranch blind to support a gambling habit."

"I don't believe that, dear. How do you know that's what the money is being used for?"

"Trust me, Mother, it is. I've seen this before." She waved her hand toward the bank statements. "Besides, he didn't deny it."

"I still don't believe it."

Amy gritted her teeth against Mother's incessant Pollyanna routine. Poor Mother, who always believed that everything would work out while being incapable of doing anything to make sure that it did.

"How can you be so sure of him so soon?" Amy asked.

"I don't really know. But *I do* know I don't see him that way."

"The pattern in the books is crystal clear," Amy said, enunciating each word precisely. "He didn't even try to hide it. Hank has been gambling his money away. I've even heard him betting with Willie."

"Well, I'll leave you to doubt the man. I like Hank. I trust him."

"Mother," Amy said dryly, "you've only known him for a couple of days."

"I'm a much better judge of character than you give me credit for. One day you will learn there is no such thing as a perfect man," she said without a trace of her usual querulousness. "You fall in love with a man because of his good qualities and you learn to tolerate the bad."

Mother struggled to her feet. "Hank is not gambling his ranch away or jeopardizing his relationship with those children. There must be another explanation."

"Why would you trust Hank more than you trust me?"

"It's not you I don't trust. It's whatever you found in there." She pointed to the stacks of paper on the desk.

"You've never really respected my work or my abilities, have you, Mother?"

Mother stepped around the desk and rested her hands on Amy's shoulders. Why did that make her feel like crying?

"I don't doubt that you do good work," Mother said, staring into her eyes. "Something happened to you when your father died. You became driven and rigid."

"I had to," Amy said, her voice hitching. "Someone had to support us."

"Yes, and you did it well. I will always be grateful for that, but those times are long gone, Amy. You shot to the top too fast. You have more than enough money. You no longer have to hedge your bets against poverty. You no longer have to be afraid to live. And to love."

Oh, but I do. People die or leave. Everyone but you.

"Learn to relax and enjoy life," Mother continued. "Learn to get close to people and stop being afraid of them."

The cramp in Amy's stomach told her the woman who knew her better than anyone else on earth had cut too close to the bone.

Mother walked to the door, then hesitated with her hand on the knob, peering at Amy over her shoulder. "Be careful when you accuse a man like Hank of something so serious. Good men are rare, sweetheart."

Alone again Amy fell into her chair and rested her elbows on the desk. She forced herself to look at the facts, to try to sort through the murky field of doubt to find the truth. Outside the office she heard the sound of children playing and Hank's laughter.

Straightening her back, she studied the numbers yet again. The facts won out. Numbers didn't lie.

The guy was gambling. For sure. She'd given him the chance to tell her it was something else, but Hank had just stared at her and told her to fix it.

When she heard Hannah call that dinner was ready, she couldn't bring herself to sit with all of those vaguely censorious faces. She knew she wouldn't be able to eat a thing, anyway.

Standing in the office doorway, she watched the children, Willie and the two teenaged camp counselors file across the hallway to the dining room. Hank brought up the rear with Cheryl in his arms. Amy felt a tug of regret that she would bring this big man down. She had no choice. If Leila wanted to realize any profit from this place, Amy was going to have to help her sell it. Now. Before Hank bet the farm on some wager he couldn't win.

"THE CAMPERS are coming home." Amy sat on a wicker chair on the veranda on Friday afternoon with Cheryl on her lap. "Look." She pointed to a dust cloud approaching from the direction of the Hungry Hollow.

The other young kids milled around the veranda, watching and waiting, too. The five horses neared the yard, escalating the excitement of the kids. An extraordinarily good-looking ranch hand led the group into the yard amid cheers from the children.

"You kids stay up here until those horses stop," Hank said to the younger ones. "I don't want anyone crying about trampled toes."

"You teach these children well," Amy said. They'd been living in an uneasy truce since yesterday, pretending that things were normal for the children's sake.

Hank turned to look at her, his expression serious. "Yep. Last thing they need is an injury sustained on my ranch."

Chatter and laughter filled the air and the campers looked dirty and tired, but happy.

"Hey, Davey," Hank called to a boy who looked to be ten or eleven. "How was the trip?"

"Great! I herded cattle with Matt." Amy recognized him as the boy she'd seen on the cowboy's lap, with equal parts terror and thrill on his face. He ran over and threw himself against Hank. "And I slept in a tent on the ground."

"On the ground?" Hank asked, grinning. "Wow."

"Yeah, and I wasn't scared when that animal came scratching around the tent."

"Probably just a raccoon."

"That's what Matt said when I woke him up."

Hank nudged Davey toward the screen door. "Go on in and get settled."

"Hi, John," Hank greeted another boy, who mumbled hello.

John, twelve years old or so, shuffled up the steps because the laces of his running shoes were undone. He walked with his legs spread and his hands in his pockets so his too-wide pants wouldn't fall down. A gray hoodie covered his hair. He frowned at both Amy and Cheryl on his way past.

"We can't help them all." Hank sounded light, philosophical, but Amy read a deep concern on his face.

A couple of boys scooted by. Cheryl's head swiveled between the kids running by and the activity in the yard.

One young girl, a nine- or ten-year-old, threw herself against Hank. "I had fun!"

"Did you, Melissa? Are you ready to bust some broncs at the rodeo with me?"

Melissa giggled, then approached Amy and Cheryl. Melissa held Cheryl's cheeks in her grubby hands and rubbed noses with her.

After Melissa ran inside, Hank crouched on his heels in front of Amy and held a finger out to Cheryl, who curled her hand around it. Amy noticed that he was careful not to touch her. Amy wasn't contagious, for heaven's sake.

"Melissa was one of the saddest kids you ever saw when she first got here," Hank said quietly. He spoke to Amy, but looked at Cheryl. He'd been like this since yesterday, subdued and unwilling to meet her eye.

"She really changed that much so quickly?" she asked.

"Yeah, I had her paired with Jenny, one of the ranch hands," he said, his expression warm. "Jenny can draw any kid out of her shell and make her love horses and ranching."

He rubbed the back of Cheryl's hand with his thumb then stood to walk down the steps.

At the bottom of the lawn, the driveway still teemed with horses and ranch hands. Amy watched as Hank greeted Jenny with a brief pat on the shoulder that signified nothing more than affection. Then Amy chastised herself for imagining that it was any of her business. It really didn't matter to her.

Hank, Willie, Jenny and the other ranch hands led the horses into the barn to unload and curry them after their ride.

Amy turned and went into the house with Cheryl on her arm. The kids had congregated in the living room and just before she entered the room, a child's voice rose above the chatter. "I don't like her. She was mad at Hank."

Another voice, a boy's sounding older than the first one, answered, "She better not treat him bad when I'm here. I'll punch her in the nose."

As she stood on the threshold, the kids looked at her sideways. Some of them scowled.

More enemies. It was too much. She was not a bad person. She wasn't.

One by one, they left the living room to play in the recreation room, as if Amy had cooties. When Cheryl left her to join them, Amy felt abandoned.

By the time she heard the boots of the ranch hands clomping across the porch and into the house, she was curled in an armchair alone in the room, a pariah.

A motley crew passed on their way to the dining room—cowhands dressed in hopelessly rumpled jeans and plaid or denim shirts. Not a single ironed item among the lot, but at least they were clean, having obviously taken the time to wash and change in the bunkhouse.

One of them, the impossibly good-looking cowboy she'd met on the drive home from the Hungry Hollow, stopped short to stare at her. Jenny, talking to someone behind her, bumped into his sturdy body and bounced back. He didn't budge.

A drop of water from his hair dripped onto his high cheekbone and ran past the hollow of a dimple beside his full lips to fall from his square jaw. He was one gorgeous man and he knew it.

He stepped into the room, his huge belt buckle with its bucking bronco shining in the lamplight. He grinned when he saw that she'd noticed it.

There was a lot of vanity in this guy, but his pure male appreciation warmed her when she needed it most.

"C'mon, Matt." Jenny stood in the doorway, scowling at Amy. Jenny probably had a crush on this guy. Too bad. Amy's pride was in sore need of bolstering right now.

"Matt, dinner's waiting," Jenny said with a rough edge of impatience and something that sounded like desperation.

Matt's eyes never left Amy's face. "Sure," he said. "Be there in a minute."

"Don't wait forever or you'll starve, Long."

Matt crouched on his heels in front of Amy, stretching a tanned, long-fingered hand toward her.

"Hi. Remember me? Matt Long." He grasped her hand with a firm grip and shook it.

"I'm Amy."

"I remember. You've got the prettiest voice. You must sing like an angel."

Amy smiled. God, that was corny.

He still held her hand. Amy let him.

Someone nearby cleared his throat.

"Sorry, just gonna tape *Jeopardy!* for Gladys." Amy realized that Hank had arrived and she hadn't even noticed.

She sensed him walking to the rec room, and tried to pull her hand out of Matt's grasp.

Suddenly she didn't want Hank to think she was the kind of woman who fell for a man like Matt. She usually wasn't.

A minute later, she felt Hank's return. "You both might want to come and eat before it gets cold." A hint of something—sadness?—rang in his voice.

Matt's intent gaze never left Amy's face. "Be there in a minute, Hank."

Amy tugged on her hand and Matt let it go this time. She realized he'd been staking his claim in front of Hank and that angered her. Enough that she turned down Matt's offer to escort her to the table.

"I'll see you after dinner then." Matt stood and left the room with a megawatt smile.

Amy sat back in her chair. She hadn't been hit with such a wave of lust since the first time she'd seen Tony standing in the Blues Haven doorway looking like a Greek idol—tall, handsome and supremely confident—who knocked her off her aching, overworked waitressing feet.

Tony. The name had a sobering effect. The reality of her situation struck her full force. She was in no shape to start a flirtation, but she wanted to. Oh, how she wanted to—to feel beautiful, to feel those first excited impulses of a new infatuation and to know her own power with the opposite sex.

She wasn't interested in another Tony, though—vain, conceited and too shallow to stand by a woman when she needed him most.

She spent the rest of the night in her attic room avoiding everyone, particularly Matt and her own confused feelings for Hank. It was the coward's way out and she didn't care.

HANK SAT BESIDE GLADYS on the sofa. Alex Trebek read another clue from the board and Gladys answered correctly before any of the contestants rang their buzzers.

Hank drummed his fingers on the arm of the sofa.

He couldn't stand the tension any longer.

He paused the tape.

Gladys turned to him with a frown that matched the one he'd seen on her daughter's face so many times.

"I need to ask you something," he said.

Gladys nodded.

"Um…I don't know for sure how to say it," he temporized. Great word.

"Hank," Gladys said quietly, "just ask."

"Why would Amy think I was a gambler?"

"She said it had something to do with a pattern she saw in your bank statements." She pulled the collar of her robe up around her neck.

"You cold?" Hank asked.

"A little."

Hank pulled an afghan from the armchair and draped it around her shoulders.

"Thanks," she said. "Don't ask me exactly what it was that Amy found. I'm sure you understand those things a lot better than I do."

Don't count on it.

"But I'm not a gambler," he said.

"I know that, Hank," Gladys answered.

"You do?" he asked. Jeez, why would Gladys trust him while her daughter wouldn't?

"You aren't the kind of man to gamble."

Hank stretched his arm along the back of the sofa. "How do you know?"

"I married one." She patted his leg. "I know that you aren't."

Hank smiled. The woman's faith in him felt good. So…Amy's father had been a gambler.

That didn't tell him what Amy had found that led her to believe that *Hank* was a gambler. What kind of mistake was he making with the finances that would lead to that assumption? If he told her he wasn't a gambler, would she then turn around and figure out the truth on her own?

Could he find out from her without revealing his real problem?

He was going to have to try. He couldn't stand having Amy look at him with disappointment for one more day.

"Excuse me, Gladys," he said, "there's something I have to do."

He restarted *Jeopardy!*, then headed upstairs to Amy's bedroom.

CHAPTER EIGHT

STANDING ON THE LANDING in front of Amy's door, Hank wiped his sweaty palms on his thighs, then he knocked on the door.

He heard rustling inside, then the door opened and there she stood tying the sash of a silky, flowery robe.

Don't tie it up. Take it off.

Whoa. Where had that thought come from?

Her hair was mussed and about as sexy as anything he'd ever seen. She tucked a strand behind her ear.

"I'll do that." Cripes, he'd said it out loud.

"What?" she asked.

"Nothing," he mumbled.

The urge to touch her nearly overwhelmed him. He shoved his hands into his pockets.

"Did I wake you?" he whispered, even though there was no way he could possibly wake any of the kids on the second floor.

She shook her head.

"I need to ask you something." He cracked the

knuckles of his right hand. Damn, he was nervous. "How come you thought I was a gambler?"

Her lips thinned. "Are you telling me that you aren't?"

"I'm not."

She looked confused, as if not sure what to believe.

"What did you see in those bank statements that made you think I was?"

"Large sums of money withdrawn from your account weekly, with no record of where it was going."

"You thought I was a gambler because I take money out all the time?" Was *that* all? He laughed.

She frowned. "There's no record of where the money is going."

"Come here," he said and grabbed her hand. It felt small and cool in his as he led her down the stairs and into his bedroom.

Pulling open the drawer of his bedside table, he yanked out stacks of bill payment receipts—for utilities, phone, cable—and threw them onto the bed.

"That's what I take the money out for."

Amy rifled through them. "These are all stamped Paid."

"That's right. I pay them in person."

She stared at him, a hint of color in her one

cheek. Embarrassment at having misjudged him, maybe?

"I've been searching for these all over that hellhole you call a desk," she said.

Hank swallowed. Nope, not embarrassment. Anger.

"Hank, these are the kinds of things I need to know if I'm going to figure out how things work on this ranch."

Hank shrugged. "Sorry," he said. *Sheepishly. Really* good word for how he was feeling.

Amy frowned at the stacks on the bed. "This doesn't account for all of it."

"C'mon," he said and took her to the first floor.

Just inside the living room, he pulled open the drawer of a black credenza. Stacks and stacks of twenties sat inside, held neatly in piles with elastic bands.

"What are you doing with so much cash in the house?" she asked, staring at him like he'd grown a second head.

"I pay the ranch hands out of this."

"You pay them in cash? Under the table?"

"What do you mean, under the table?"

"What about your payroll taxes? Don't you pay those?"

"Donna at the bank does all of that for me."

"The bank does it for you?"

Hank smiled. "This is a small town, Amy. They

do things like that here. Donna moonlights for a lot of other people, too, when they need help. We're ranchers, not accountants."

Amy studied the piles of cash. "Do your employees know this money is here?"

Hank shrugged. "Sure."

Amy placed a fist on her hip and eyed him sternly. "You are asking to be robbed blind. How do you know they aren't helping themselves to a few bucks when they walk through here?"

"You know what you have to understand here, Amy?" He jabbed his index finger toward her.

She backed away, her movement subtle but unmistakable.

Hank took a deep breath and evened out his temper. He never intimidated people. What was it about this woman that got under his skin?

"You have to recognize," he said, "that this isn't the city. These people are more than employees. They're family. I trust every last one of them."

She looked into his eyes, then nodded. "Okay, Hank. I understand." She plowed one hand through her hair, took a deep breath and held it. It did great things to her breasts. He tried not to stare.

"I'm so sorry," she whispered, "for thinking you were a gambler. I let my emotions overcome my professional judgment."

"Aw, hey, that's okay," Hank said. He was so

damn happy to have her look at him without disappointment.

She glanced down at their linked hands. He did, too, surprised to realize he hadn't let go of her hand since he'd taken hold of it outside of her attic door. It felt like it belonged with his.

He rubbed his thumb across her knuckles.

Her one cheek turned pink and he wanted to lick it, to turn it redder, then move to the other pale cheek and warm it with a kiss.

With a short tug, she pulled her hand free. Placed a hand against her chest. Cleared her throat. She looked as rattled as he felt.

As she stepped past him into the hall, a light floral scent drifted by.

"You're going to leave the money there and keep paying the ranch hands in cash, aren't you?" she asked, her smile rueful.

"You can't change a zebra's stripes," he said, his tone matching hers.

Heading upstairs, she mounted a few steps, then glanced at him over her shoulder, her blond hair gilded by a table lamp glowing in the hallway, the curves of her hips and bum lovingly outlined by ivory silk. He just about ran after her to carry her to his bedroom and make love to her on that stack of bills she'd gotten so riled about.

She smiled and said good-night.

As he watched her disappear, Hank thought, you can't change a cowboy's desire.

Amy Graves, what are you doing to my heart?

But he knew there was no hope for him with her.

He rubbed his chest and turned away.

ON SATURDAY afternoon, the knock on the door echoed the pounding in Amy's head. She'd been in the office for hours, updating the accounts with the bills from Hank's bedroom. Her stomach grumbled. She'd missed lunch. Stretching her arms above her head, she rolled the kinks out of her neck.

"Come in," she called.

Hank opened the door and leaned in. "We opened the pool. Everyone's going swimming."

A small head peeked around the door—Cheryl, with her wide eyes full of hope.

Hank shrugged, then asked quietly, "Can she stay with you? She won't go in the pool."

Amy nodded. After Hank left, she asked, "Why won't you go in the pool, Cheryl?"

"I can't swim." Cheryl flicked the nails of her index fingers across each other. She was always calm—fatalistic, almost. Signs of nerves in the child were cause for worry.

"Are you afraid to go swimming?"

Cheryl nodded. She pushed the door open all the way and crossed the room to stand beside Amy.

How unfortunate that Cheryl was going to miss out on one of the great joys in life because of her fear.

Amy took in all the work she had to do then looked at Cheryl.

"Cheryl, if I take you into the pool, will you try swimming?"

The child shrugged. "I'm 'fraid."

"I know." Amy hugged her close. "It's good to try to get over fears to have fun in life, though. We'll stay in the shallow end and I'll hold you up every minute, okay?"

Cheryl let out a small sigh. "'Kay."

Amy left Cheryl in her bedroom to get into her bathing suit, then ran upstairs and undressed. Drawing her courage around her, she looked at herself in the mirror. The scar on her chest where her right breast used to be still shocked her. She spun away from the image, then put on the bathing suit Leila had warned her to pack.

A high-necked red one-piece with a wide ruffle around the top, the suit was more comfortable than any she'd ever owned before. The last time she'd worn one had been more than two years ago. She tucked her prosthesis into the pocket hidden by the ruffle.

Studying herself in the mirror, she thought she looked all right. Normal. No one would know one of her breasts was fake.

Impatient with her own shallowness, she turned away from the mirror and grabbed a white terry-cloth robe from the bed. At least she was alive, and finally healthy. She headed down to the second floor to get Cheryl, who appeared in the hall in a silver one-piece suit with fuzzy brown monkeys climbing a coconut tree on the front. It looked brand-new. And cheap.

"I like your suit, Cheryl. It's very pretty."

Cheryl rubbed her chest and stomach. "Mommy bought it for me."

"Let's get some sunscreen on before we head out."

The din filtering through the screen door at the back of the house increased as they approached. They stepped into the sunshine, amid the screams, laughter and sounds of splashing, then through the gate in the chain link fence that surrounded the pool area. The water at the deep end churned with waves, arms and legs, and naked heads.

Hank held a volleyball above his head in the water while a bunch of kids tried to wrestle it away from him. Judging by the grin on his face, he was in his element.

Amy smiled, headed to the shallow end with Cheryl and dumped their towels on a deck lounger.

Matt waved from the other end of the deck, gave her the once-over and wiggled his eyebrows.

Amy touched her neckline to make sure everything was covered, but Matt had already returned his focus to the kids in the water.

Leaning down to look Cheryl in the eye, Amy said, "You stand right here on the side of the pool and I'll lift you into the water after I get in. Okay?"

Amy went over the side into the water and shivered. Dunking her head under, she came up laughing. "It's chilly but wonderful. Refreshing." She patted the side of the pool. "Sit down here."

Cheryl sat on the edge of the pool, keeping her feet out of the water.

Grasping Cheryl under her arms, Amy picked her up and slid her off the side, dipping her feet and legs into the water. Cheryl recoiled, but Amy continued to ease her into the pool.

Cheryl shivered. "Do you know how to swim, Amy?"

"Yes." Amy wrapped her arms around Cheryl. "I used to swim at home for exercise."

"Are you really, really good?" Cheryl's voice shook.

"I'll keep you safe," Amy murmured in her ear.

She spooned handfuls of water onto Cheryl's shoulders while holding her closely until she felt the child's shivers ease. Swirling the girl through the water, Amy continued to hold her beneath the arms, never letting her fall farther than waist deep.

As Cheryl began to relax, she ran her fingers through the water, making small waves on the surface.

A sharp whistle split the air. Cheryl flung her arms and legs around Amy and clung like a little monkey. Spinning around, Amy saw Matt, who stood at the side of the pool, blow his whistle again. The water churned as swimmers hauled themselves out of the pool, climbing the sides or the steps. She quickly followed suit.

Once she and Cheryl were on the deck, Amy spied Hank pulling himself out at the far end. The muscles in his arms and large shoulders rippled. Water sluiced from his strong back. He wore a pair of black trunks that fit snugly around a tight behind. His legs were long, well-shaped and covered with brown hair.

Hank Shelter had a beautiful body. Amy felt a flutter in her chest and the familiar confusion she experienced around Hank.

"Roll call!" Hank yelled. He held a clipboard and checked off names as the children called them out. Matt peered into the clear water of the pool and nodded, satisfied that it was empty.

Attendance completed, Hank picked up an oversize tube of sunscreen, and applied it to the kids in the lineup. Once lathered, they each chose a toy from a large plastic hamper, then jumped into the pool. A couple of boys started diving for hockey pucks. Others grabbed pool noodles to float. An older girl sat on the lip of the pool, inflating something large and green. As it grew and took shape, Cheryl pointed. "Look. It's a alligator."

Her fascination with the alligator allowed Amy to get her back in the water with no shivers or fears.

The girl who blew the toy was the same one who had rubbed noses with Cheryl. Melissa. Amy was slowly learning their names. She'd noticed that Hank never forgot or mixed them up.

Melissa slid into the pool and swam over to Cheryl, pushing the inflated alligator ahead of her.

"Want to go for a ride, Cheryl? Get on."

The alligator had an indentation just about the right size for a child's bum. Amy lifted Cheryl into it and she rested her head on the back of the 'gator's head and her feet along his tail. Melissa propelled Cheryl gently around the water. Another girl joined her and drifted on the other side of the float. Cheryl lay on the crocodile like a little princess.

Amy's chest tightened. How had Cheryl survived the ravages of cancer? The chemotherapy? The dread? Was she afraid of death? Did she even understand the concept? With what she'd been through Cheryl deserved every speck of pampering she got here on the ranch.

Amy pulled herself out of the pool to sit on the side, adjusting the neckline of her bathing suit, making sure it didn't dip too low. Hank and Matt weren't the only men around the pool. Two more stood on the other side, keeping eagle eyes on the children.

Keep them safe.

A boy suddenly jostled the alligator, tossing Cheryl into the water.

"Hey!" Melissa yelled.

Amy was in the water like a cannon shot, swimming for Cheryl and grabbing her, pushing her head above water.

"Cheryl," she cried. "Cheryl."

Cheryl came up coughing and choking.

"Are you all right, honey?" Amy's heart rate shot through the stratosphere as she held Cheryl's head forward and patted the child's back.

Holding Cheryl's shaking body close brought memories of clasping other trembling limbs, the bent head…it all felt bone-chillingly familiar.

She could swear she could smell cabbage rolls.

Of course. That was the meal Mother had put in the oven an hour before Dad died. That horrid day Dad lay on the floor of the living room, unmoving, his head on Amy's knees.

Mother had opened the front door. Three fire-fighters ran in.

When the younger one crouched beside Amy

and eased Dad's head to the floor, she smelled smoke on the man's boots and sweet cologne on his neck. She wanted to tell him it was too strong.

They began to work on her dad, attempting to revive him but their actions seemed rushed, almost brutal.

"Be careful," she cried.

"Shh, it's okay. She's okay."

She?

Warm arms wrapped around Amy from behind. When she looked over her shoulder, she saw that it was Hank. Instead of cabbage rolls, she smelled chlorine. She was in the swimming pool at the Sheltering Arms with Cheryl clutching her as kids laughed and yelled nearby.

She inhaled and found a warm strength in Hank's arms that she desperately needed.

He propelled them toward the ladder at the corner of the pool. Once they were settled there, he asked, "What happened?"

"Someone knocked Cheryl off the alligator." Amy's voice shook. "She could have drowned."

"I don't think so," Hank answered, his smile grim. He gestured with his head toward Cheryl. Amy understood right away. He didn't want Cheryl upset.

"Do you want to go back on the alligator?" she asked, trying to make her voice sound normal.

Cheryl cuddled into Amy's shoulder and shook

her head. Amy could kick herself for transmitting her own fear to the girl.

She glanced at Hank and lifted her shoulders in a small shrug.

He pulled himself out of the pool, shoulder and back muscles rippling with the effort, then turned and took Cheryl from Amy's arms. He stretched a hand to help Amy out. Pausing only to grab towels for each of them, he held on to her hand while he led them into the house and up the stairs.

Was there no end to this man's strength?

He gestured for Amy to enter the attic room ahead of him then handed Cheryl to her.

"Take her suit off and get her dry."

He rummaged in the dresser and pulled out one of Amy's T-shirts. Expensive silk. Amy didn't care—simply put it on Cheryl, then nestled her under the quilt.

"Nap now, okay?"

Cheryl nodded. "You, too?"

Amy nodded. Cheryl's eyes drifted closed.

She felt the heat of Hank behind her and slowly turned. If she was getting into the bed with Cheryl, she had to change.

"You okay?" Hank asked. "You look pale."

"I'm fine." The tremor in her voice betrayed her. "It…it brought back memories of Dad's death. I don't know why."

She seemed to be living a life of heightened

emotions these days and they left her baffled. Unsettled.

"I urged her to go in the pool. I told her it was good to face down fears."

Her throat tightened. She put her hand on Hank's chest, her remorse needing release. "Oh, Hank, I told her I would keep her safe."

"Poor Amy," Hank said, and ran a thumb across her cheek. It drifted to her mouth while he stared at her lips, his eyes dark as roasted hazelnuts in the dim room. The sun had drifted around to the other side of the house. Hank's big body blocked the light from the window.

He became a mass of shadows and contours, scents—lemon, spice and chlorine—and his ever-present, all-surrounding heat.

He grabbed her hand, tugged her from the bedroom and closed the door with a restrained click. A barely controlled burn emanated from him.

"Amy," he said, his rough voice reverberating with need and desire. "I have to do this."

He cradled the back of her head and pressed her against the wall. She grabbed his shoulders, the skin smooth and hot under her palms.

He swooped down, pressed his full lips to hers, then washed her mouth with his tongue, invaded every corner, and all Amy could think was, *yes!*

A powerful arm wrapped around her waist and pulled her against his body. Amy's head swam.

She pressed against him, the moisture in their wet suits warming. She felt the bloom of long-gone desire, felt a swell of hard warmth at her belly, and exulted. Images of his body under her hands flew through her and she wanted everything: Hank's generosity of spirit and the massive strength and weight of him on top of her, and the burgeoning wonder, full and thick, she knew she would find under his black suit, and the sheer delight of caressing him while she sent him spinning higher with desire. Making love with him would be nothing short of spectacular.

A dizzying maelstrom of colored stars burst through her mind. Unsteady, she grasped him around the neck, leaned into him to obliterate every atom of space between them, and grabbed a handful of thick, wet hair.

He moaned.

Oh, Hank.

She knew that she'd needed to put her hands on him since the first time she'd seen him covered with children and laughing.

His hand touched her breast and her nipple peaked. She fell away from his kiss and closed her eyes. His lips wrapped around her nipple and her eyes flew open. He'd pulled her suit down off her left shoulder. She looked down at the head of the man suckling at her naked breast and threaded her fingers through his chestnut hair.

She lifted the streak of caramel, soft between her fingers.

Electricity shot from her breast through her belly to her groin and she reveled in it, all of it new, powerful, profound.

Oh, Hank.

His hand caressed her other breast through the damp fabric. She felt nothing. *Nothing.*

Oh, God. The wrong breast. She gasped and pulled away. No! She couldn't let him touch her, let him find out, have him look at her with disgust.

She grasped the fabric over her prosthesis, held fast and hard so he wouldn't move it.

He looked at her with his dark eyes glazed with desire. For her. No, not for her. For a whole woman.

"I can't." Her voice cracked with disappointment in the destruction of her femininity, her life, her dreams.

She knew what men thought of scarred women. Hank shook his head, still looking dazed.

"What?" he asked, his breath hot on her face.

"I can't do this." She ached, wept, tried to step away. He wouldn't let her.

"You want this as much as I do." His thumb rubbed across the aroused nipple of her bare breast, her good one.

She slammed her hand over his and removed it from her body.

"Why not?" He bent toward her to kiss her again.

She pushed him away.

"I don't understand you," Hank murmured. "Do you want me or don't you?"

She couldn't tell him the truth. "I don't want you."

It sounded like a patent lie to her own ears, but Hank believed her and retreated. His face lost all expression, but not before she saw a flash of pain.

"Then what was all of this about?" he asked.

"A moment of weakness on my part," she whispered. She tried to touch him, to soothe his pain, but he stepped farther away. She winced.

"It isn't you, Hank," she whispered. "It's me."

"Yeah, I've gotten that line before," Hank said with uncharacteristic bitterness. He turned and raced down the stairs.

Amy slid along the wall until she sat on the floor, her breasts cradled in her hands, one bare and the other clothed in fabric and shame.

She remembered Tony's reaction to her altered body.

The worst time, the absolute worst, had come after she'd already had her mastectomy. She'd stood in front of the bathroom mirror, her image shimmering through her tears.

Her chest had lost its perfect symmetry. On one side, a beautiful breast. On the other, a scar still swollen and red where a matching breast used to be.

A movement in the doorway caught her attention. Tony stood behind her, his gaze locked on the mirror. The revulsion on his face shocked her. Shame flooded through her. She snatched the lapels of her robe and wrapped them around herself, left her arms crossed over her chest to protect herself from Tony's horror.

Where was the man she'd thought she'd married? Where was his compassion, his love for her?

Oh, why hadn't she locked the door? But that would only have delayed the inevitable. Tony was going to have to see her at some point.

How many times early in their marriage had Tony urged her to stop wearing a bra? After all, he'd say, why mess with perfection?

Why? To save her life, of course.

He'd never touched her again.

Amy dragged herself into her room, changed into a sweat suit and crawled under the quilt with Cheryl, chilled to the soul in spite of the warmth of the breeze wafting through the window.

LATE IN THE AFTERNOON, a knock awakened Amy. She slid out of bed without disturbing Cheryl, rubbing her gritty eyes, and opened the door.

Matt leaned one shoulder against the wall and grinned.

"Hey," he said, his voice as smooth as chocolate.

"Hi," she whispered, brushing her hand over her hair, knowing she looked a mess and self-conscious with this gorgeous man so close.

He gestured toward the bed with his chin. "Who's your little friend?"

"Cheryl."

"She okay after her scare in the pool?"

"I think so."

"You going to the dance tonight?" he asked.

"What dance?"

"Didn't Hank tell you about it?"

She shook her head, guessing that Hank hadn't wanted to ask her on a date after what had happened this afternoon.

"It's at the Legion in town. Everyone's going. Kids, too."

Everyone? Even the children? But apparently not her. Oh, Hank, that hurt.

Matt leaned his forearm high on the wall, flexing his biceps. "I want you to come with me. My truck's a whole lot more comfortable than the old school bus Hank uses."

Did Hank think she'd stay home alone? That she deserved to? She wanted to go out, to experience a little carefree happiness. But what about Mother?

"I'd like to go, but I don't want to leave my mother here alone."

"She's going," Matt said. "I heard Hank ask her."

He'd asked Mother, but not her? That tremor of envy Amy felt about their fondness for each other erupted into a full-blown earthquake, even if it didn't make sense, given what had happened between her and Hank this afternoon.

Matt reached out to tuck a strand of hair behind her ear. A callus scraped across her earlobe and she shivered. He shouldn't be touching her so intimately, but she didn't complain, off balance from her encounter with Hank and still half asleep.

"All right," she said. "I'll go with you."

"Seven o'clock. At the front door."

She nodded.

"It's a date." He flashed her a dazzling smile, then left.

A date, but not with Hank.

CHAPTER NINE

SHE REALLY DIDN'T WANT to go with Matt. Instead, she wanted to be with Mother and Hank and Cheryl and the other children.

Amy's stomach jittered as she tucked her raw silk blouse into black jeans then slipped her feet into black shoes—not at the thought of going out with Matt, but with apprehension about her next encounter with Hank.

Mother sat on the bed in Amy's room, her navy-blue dress with the white polka dots neatly pressed, her hair and face shining. Soft pink lipstick shone on her lips.

"That looks nice, Amy," she said.

Amy straightened the button tab of her shirt until it aligned with the exact center of her pants. Laying a hand on her flat stomach, she pressed, hoping to stop the fluttering.

"You look pretty," Cheryl said from her perch on the neatly made bed. She sat cross-legged wearing a pair of faded blue jeans and a pink sweater.

Amy turned from their reflections in the mirror and smiled. "Thank you. So do you. Should I add earrings?" Amy asked. "What do you think?" She must be more nervous than she'd thought, if she was asking a child for clothing advice. Why was she so worried about what Hank would think?

Lordy, woman, get yourself together.

She opened her small jewelry box and set it on the bed between Cheryl and Mother. She stirred the contents with her finger.

"What do you think? The black stones? The danglers?"

"Those," Cheryl said, pointing.

"The pearls? They're a bit dressy."

"I like them." Cheryl knelt on the bed so she could see herself in the mirror. Picking up one of the pearl earrings, she held it against her earlobe, covering the small gold ball in her ear, tilting her head one way then the other.

"Pretty." She set the earring back down in the box, but left one finger touching it, reluctant to let it go.

Amy studied the child's clothes—the cheap sweater, the worn jeans—and made an impulsive decision.

"Would you like to wear these tonight?" Even as the words left her mouth, she knew she was crazy to think them, let alone say them aloud. She was offering real pearls to a child. She was certifiable, no doubt about it, but something stirred in her chest when Cheryl perked up.

Sitting up straight, she stared at Amy with large eyes and her mouth hanging open, then picked up the earrings with reverence.

"Here," Amy said, "let me put them on for you." She took off Amy's small fake gold studs, then slipped the pearls through the child's earlobes, where they shone too conspicuously on Cheryl's bald head.

"Do I look pretty like you?" Cheryl asked, hope making her dark eyes huge.

The back of Amy's eyes stung. She nodded, unable to speak.

Amy lifted Cheryl from the bed so she could look at herself in the mirror. "Let's go see if anyone else is ready." She set Cheryl on her feet.

Cheryl ran down the stairs, but Gladys stopped Amy with a hand on her arm.

"Why are you going to the dance with that randy young cowboy?"

"Because he asked me to," Amy answered, turning away from the disapproval on her mother's face. "Hank didn't even tell me about the dance."

"I'm sure that was a simple oversight."

Amy refused to answer that statement and started down the stairs, but Mother stopped her again.

"What's wrong, Amy?"

I've fallen for a man and can't have him.
"Nothing," Amy said and ran down to the first
floor, her temples pounding with every footfall.

In the foyer, Hank stood with Willie in the
middle of a crowd of children. When he saw
Cheryl descending, his eyes lit up and his cheeks
creased with a smile. Cheryl wove her way
through the children.

"Hank, Hank," she cried, "look what Amy
gived me to wear tonight."

She jumped into Hank's open arms, turning
her head this way and that to show him the
earrings.

"That was real nice of Amy."

Cheryl nodded. "Do I look pretty?"

"You look downright beautiful, darlin'."

The way he looked at Amy when he mouthed
"Thank you" sent a chill through her. She'd never
seen his eyes so cold before.

She nodded in return, continuing to stare at
him.

When Hank rested his head on top of Cheryl's,
the light glinted from his freshly washed hair and
highlighted the streak of caramel. His beige
chinos and pale blue shirt molded to the muscles
she'd caressed only hours ago.

He picked up a pure white Stetson from the
table beside the front door and set it onto Cheryl's

head. Her face disappeared. She looked like a hat on a skinny neck. Even at this distance, Amy heard her giggle.

Hank grinned and lifted the hat from Cheryl's head, then set it on his own. He looked good. Too good. Amy couldn't seem to stop staring.

The front door opened and Matt stepped into the house. When he saw Amy standing on the bottom stair, he whistled.

"Looks like I'm heading to the dance with the prettiest woman in the state."

Hank's head shot around to stare at Matt then swung her way. Emotions Amy couldn't read crossed his face, but one thing was clear: he wasn't happy. Obviously Matt hadn't told Hank they were going together. Or maybe Hank was angry because Matt had told her about the dance.

Strutting his way through the kids, Matt approached Amy, his gaze traveling her body, head to toe. He took her hand, and twirled her around and under his arm to get a look at her from all angles. He pulled her close, warmth radiating from his body through hers. She wanted to push him away, but wouldn't with everyone watching.

"You smoke, babe," he whispered for her ears only. "You're a stick of dynamite waiting for the right match to set you on fire."

The man was smooth, too smooth—not her type at all—but she was committed for the night.

She had to see this through to the end. Maybe she could leave early if her headache got any worse.

The kids filed out of the house behind Hank, Gladys and Hannah, then boarded an old yellow school bus. Matt escorted Amy to the black Jeep parked behind it, then helped her in.

When Matt climbed into the driver's seat, the cologne he'd applied with a heavy hand filled the small interior, cloying compared to the lighter lemon aftershave Hank used.

She stared at the road ahead, willing her thoughts away from Hank.

Matt took off in a spray of gravel and Amy's back hit the seat. Accelerating, he passed the slow-moving bus, honking.

He laughed. "Passed her like she was standing still."

"Who was driving?"

"Jenny."

"What's she like?"

Matt frowned. "She's just a kid."

Not such a kid. She has a full-blown crush on you, Amy thought, a very adult crush, but she didn't say it out loud. Matt had a healthy enough ego as it was. He didn't need her to tell him about the women who loved him.

They pulled up in front of the Legion Hall off Main Street in Ordinary. Cars lined the street on both sides. People walked along the sidewalks, waving and greeting each other. Amy felt a twinge of regret that she wasn't part of this warm-spirited community.

"It sure is a popular event," she said.

"Yep. There are a couple of dances every year." He took her elbow as she got out of the Jeep, his hand warm through the silk of her blouse. "Whole community turns out."

The sound of fiddles and banjos flowed out of the hall along with the light streaming through the open door.

"Country music?" she asked.

"It's a country dance, with a caller, like at a square dance."

"I don't know how to square dance."

He pulled her to him and grinned. "You just follow me."

The floor was already dense with people in square formations and following the singsong directions of the female caller to live music played full volume.

Matt's hand was too heavy on her waist and she said, "Let's dance. Show me how to do this." She prayed there would be no slow songs.

He flashed her a huge grin and pulled her onto the floor. She dipped, twirled and stumbled her way through the steps until she was breathless.

The band changed tempo to a country-and-western heartbreaker. Matt pulled her flush against him and she regretted the impulse that had made her accept his invitation.

She scanned the crowd over his shoulder until she found Hank. He had a pretty woman in his arms. They talked quietly and laughed.

As Amy jerked Matt's hand from her buttock to her waist, she envied the woman who had Hank's attention. She could have been that woman tonight if she was whole. She cursed fate even as she tugged at Matt's wandering hand again.

Matt twirled her off the dance floor. "I gotta visit the men's room. Don't go anywhere."

She was going to go somewhere, all right, if Matt didn't start keeping his hands to himself.

Heading for the refreshment table, she was stopped by countless people introducing themselves. She'd never felt so welcome in a community before and it warmed her. She filled a cup with pink punch and tasted it. Too sweet and fruity. What she needed was a shot of really good Scotch.

She felt Hank's presence before she saw him and turned around slowly. He stood behind her with his expression shuttered and a question on his lips.

"Why, Amy?"

"Why what?" she asked, but she knew.

"What does Matt have that I don't? Good looks?"

Her heart sank and she hated that he might think she was that shallow. "Nothing could be further from the truth."

"Is it because I'm not smart, not college or university educated?"

Before she could answer, he plowed on. "Neither is Matt."

She put a hand on his arm to stop him and he flinched away from her. "It isn't you, Hank," she said. "The problem really, truly, is with me."

"What exactly is the problem?" he asked, belligerence creeping in.

Amy felt her traitorous right cheek heat up. She couldn't possibly tell him about her breast. How on earth would she even phrase it? How could she confess that to a man she only barely knew?

That thought stopped her. She'd only met Hank this week, yet she felt like she knew as much as any woman would need to know—that he was kind, strong, ethical and sexy. She realized that Hank had no idea how appealing he was, but she knew. She ached to place her hand on his chest, to cover his heart and feel the pulse surge strong and invincible through his veins, to believe that this man would never leave a woman once he'd committed to her.

The bottom line, though? He would not find her chest the least bit attractive, and someday, even this big, strong giant would die.

She shook her head, stricken by a sense of loss.

Turning from Hank, she searched the room for a bar and spotted one in the far corner.

Before she reached it, Matt caught up to her. "Hey, you in the mood for a little drinking?"

Amy nodded, too overwhelmed with sorrow to answer. Matt returned with a beer. She hated beer. *What the hell,* she thought and took a long swig. All she needed was alcohol's numbing effect. It didn't matter what form it came in.

She took another big gulp.

"Whoa, slow down there, Amy." Matt took her nearly empty bottle and set it on a table beside his. "The night's still young. Let's dance."

He twirled her into another set. Toward the end of the dance, she noticed Hank talking to an attractive woman a little older than herself.

Matt saw her watching Hank. "That's Macy Allen," he said. "Used to be Hank's wife."

Hank's wife? Of course. He'd had a son, so he was probably married at some point. Amy studied Macy. About Hank's age. Slim. A little soft around the middle. Pretty in a mild sort of way.

"What happened?" she asked, turning back to Matt.

"She left after Hank turned the Lucky S into the Sheltering Arms. Said if she'd wanted to live with a saint, she'd have married Mother Teresa."

"What a mean thing to say to a great guy like Hank."

"Hey, Macy's not a bad person. Just couldn't watch all these sick little kids come to the ranch when her own baby was dead."

"Oh. Of course. Poor woman."

A tall man with a mustache and a brown cowboy hat took Macy's arm, nodded to Hank then led her away.

"Macy's current husband, Albert. Mayor of Ordinary," Matt said. "Owns the first ranch on the other side of town."

She wanted to know more, but the fiddle started a lively tune and the dancers twirled. She tried in vain to keep track of Hank, but lost him in the crowd.

At the end of that dance, she headed for the bar. Matt bought her another beer, then pointed to the belt buckle he wore.

"Hey, did I tell you how I got this buckle?" He rattled on about some rodeo, but Amy tuned him out.

She drank her beer. It went to her head but did nothing to ease her sadness. Here she was at a dance where she should be having fun, but she was with the wrong man. The right man was in this room, but about as far away from her as a man could get. She could never indulge her desire for him.

At that moment, she spotted Hank near the door with Cheryl sitting on his arm. The man looked right holding a child. He should have had a bunch of his own. He and Macy should have tried for more. Maybe then he wouldn't have had to bring children to his ranch.

Who was Amy kidding? Hank was born to bring these children to his ranch. Even if he'd had his own, there was so much love in the man's heart, he had plenty of room for more. And more. And more.

And the children loved him. How many children had he influenced with that love? Probably hundreds.

Hank's gaze zoned in on Amy as if he'd felt her stare. His eyes were shadowed by the blazing white hat, but she knew them by heart.

Without warning, Matt pulled her onto the dance floor again and her head spun. When she could finally look back to where Hank had stood, he was gone and Amy's sense of loss was staggering.

MATT PARKED the Jeep behind the stables, between the school bus and Amy's Audi.

A faint glow from the light on the side of the building filtered through tree limbs to barely illuminate Matt as he turned to Amy. His arm snaked across the back of her seat while his other hand settled on her waist, surprising her. He'd been surprising her with his too-fast moves since Hank and the children had left the dance.

The beers she'd drunk—she'd lost count after the third—slowed her reaction. Her head felt *muzzy*. Weird word. She'd just made it up. Hank would like it.

"Let's do something about setting this stick of dynamite on fire," Matt murmured.

Before Amy could even think the word *no,* let alone say it, Matt's lips were on hers. The man could kiss. He made a fine art of it, coaxing her mouth open with gentle, persuasive licks.

He leaned into her, covering her with his muscular bulk and trailing kisses down her neck. Funny that they weren't kindling a spark, let alone setting her on fire. Maybe it was the alcohol that made her feel so detached, like this was happening to someone else.

His hand moved from her waist, easing up onto her blouse, to her breast.

"You have great breasts," he murmured.

Breasts. No, not two. Only one. Before she could stop him, his hand was on her prosthesis, kneading it as expertly as he had her real breast.

Like a startled deer, she was out of his arms, pushing him to his own side of the vehicle. Couldn't he tell the difference between a real breast and a fake one? A bitter laugh caught in her throat.

"Huh?" He shook his head, dazed, his eyes unfocused with arousal.

"I'm sorry. I can't do this." She owed him an apology for not stopping him sooner. She wasn't—had never been—a tease. "I'm truly sorry, but I can't do this."

"Why not?" He tried to reach for her again. "You want to."

Yes, but not with you. With Hank.

She pressed her hands against Matt's chest, maintaining the distance. The poor guy looked puzzled. She didn't blame him.

Fumbling for the door handle, she said, "I have to go."

"Hey, wait. I don't understand."

She leaned in after she fumbled her way out of the car. "Matt, you're an attractive man. I can't explain. Just believe me. It wouldn't work."

"What wouldn't work?" she heard him say as she walked away. He opened his door. "This isn't a relationship. It's just a little sex!"

She started to run. That was the problem. Even if she could handle the relationship, the hellish embarrassment of the sex was beyond her. Even if she had the nerve to start something with Hank, she would always be confronted with this insurmountable truth. Her body was deeply flawed, and she didn't have a clue how to tell him that.

With a man like Matt, there was no touching and holding without sex. Right now, she desperately needed to be held. Only held.

The tears stayed at bay until she entered the house, but tore out of her on the second floor, long before she made it to the safety of the attic. Sobs escaped—all the bitterness from Tony's betrayal now released in a flood of misery. He had taken one look at her scar and had never touched her again. Six months later, he'd asked for a divorce.

HANK COULDN'T UNDERSTAND why sleep eluded him until he heard Amy running past his bedroom door. He'd been waiting for her to come home. He'd wanted her home early, without Matt, so he could avoid imagining what she might be doing with the handsome cowboy.

He sat up in bed when he heard the first sob. He stood when he heard the second one and was pulling on his pants before she made it up the attic stairs. Oh, boy. She must have heard about Cheryl losing one of those earrings. He'd better make it right with her.

He found her facedown across her bed, crying like the world was coming to an end. He'd had a feeling the pearl was real. How the heck was he going to pay for it?

"Aw, Amy, please don't cry."

She rolled over and she blinked in the light from the small bedside lamp.

"What— What are you doing here?" She swiped her sleeve across her face, leaving a long smear of mascara across her cheek and a black spot on her pretty blouse. He rarely saw her less than perfectly turned out, and here she was staining her shirt. Hank's eyes nearly goggled out of his head when she wiped her nose with her sleeve. Wasn't it only diamonds that women got emotional about?

"I'm real sorry about the earring. Listen, can you stop crying? Please?" What was a man supposed to do with a weeping woman? He'd never figured that one out. He sat on the edge of the bed, let his hand linger on her shoulder.

"Earring?" Her chest rose and fell as she hiccuped. "What?"

"I'm sorry about Cheryl losing the earring. She fell asleep crying."

She started wailing again.

"Brouhaha," he mumbled. Oh, boy. What should he do?

"Oh, poor Cheryl," Amy said. "Tell her I don't care about the earring."

She didn't? Well, she sure was miserable about something. Amy hadn't really struck him as the shallow type. So what was wrong?

Matt. Of course. He could kick himself for being a fool.

His jaw hardened. "Did Matt hurt you?"

She turned a stunned face to him. "No. He isn't like that." Hiccup. "Is he?"

"I didn't think he was, but what has you so upset?"

Her face crumpled. There was no other way to describe it as sobs wrenched from somewhere deep in her body. The woman was in pain. Aw, hell.

He leaned toward her. "Do you want to tell me what this is all about?"

Without warning, she threw herself against his chest, nearly knocking him over. "I ca-a-an't. It's too *a-a-awful*."

Her breath smelled of beer. She was intoxicated. She was also an intoxicating bundle in his arms. Lord, she felt good. He breathed deeply. *Intoxicating*. Awesome word.

He wrapped his arms around her and flattened his palms on her back, on the silky fabric heated by her womanly body. It had been a long time since he'd had a woman in his arms. He didn't remember one ever feeling this good, but her pain made him miserable.

Because he had no idea what else to do to soothe her, he rocked her, like he did with the kids when they cried. But she didn't feel like a kid. She felt warm and feminine. He wanted so badly for her to turn to him for more than comfort, to pick up where they'd left off earlier.

She'd nearly destroyed him when she'd stopped his kiss. No woman had ever made him feel as good as this one did.

When her tears finally stopped, she rested limply against him, womanly and ripe in his arms even in her exhaustion. Hank tried not to think of all the things he'd love to do with her on a bed in the dark.

Forcing his mind away from images too exquisite to bear, he eased her out of his arms.

"Do you want to talk about it?"

She shook her head.

"It wasn't Matt? He didn't do anything?"

"No, he didn't do anything." The voice that had melted over him like a Chinook the day Amy had arrived at the ranch washed him with relief.

"If Matt didn't hurt you, what did?"

"I can't tell you." She faced him, her hands resting lightly on his chest, as if she didn't want to lose contact. Her touch filled him with a beautiful torture that could last all night and he would bear it. He brushed his hands up her arms for the pure pleasure of it, knowing he was taking advantage of her emotional state, knowing she wouldn't allow it if she was sober.

"I'm tired," Amy murmured. "I need to lie down."

He stopped her from drooping on top of the quilt and reached for a tissue. She wiped her eyes and blew her nose, noisily.

He took a fresh tissue, turned her face toward the small lamp that shone on the bedside table and cleaned the mascara from her cheeks.

"Don't you think you should get out of those clothes before you fall asleep?" he asked.

"No."

"Okay. At least get under the blankets to stay warm."

It was like putting a dead drunk to bed. She waited patiently for him to remove her shoes, her feet small compared to the big things he shoved into his own boots every day. For a minute, one of her feet rested in his palm and he felt a tug near his heart, and his groin, then flushed and dropped her foot.

She rested boneless against him when he stood her up to pull the sheets down. Her head fell against his shoulder and, for a moment, he set his chin on her fine hair. It smelled tropical, like mangoes or coconut. Reluctantly releasing her to end the sweet torture of holding her, he tucked her into bed—jeans, blouse and all.

He considered taking them off but couldn't bring himself to handle her with fewer clothes on—not when he couldn't touch her as he wanted to.

She fell asleep when her head hit the pillow.

He stared at her. She had secrets. What kind? Just her fear of getting close to people? Yeah, he'd already figured that one out.

There was something else—he could feel it— something she wouldn't share with him. It saddened him to no end.

Would she ever open up and tell him? The warm light traced her high cheekbone. He'd recognized her beauty that first day but had thought himself immune because she was cold, reserved. He'd learned differently since then. Amy's icy exterior was her defense against the world. Inside, she was soft, and emotional, and loving. And scared to death of getting close to people.

He sighed. Amy Graves spelled "trouble" with a capital *T.*

CHAPTER TEN

WHAT WAS THAT infernal noise splitting her head open?

Amy rolled over and realized the sound was nothing more than rain dripping from the eaves. They'd obviously had a brief shower and the sun now shone through clouds in the distance, creating four Jacob's ladders from heaven to prairie grasses. The air streaming through the open window felt hot and humid.

Sitting up gingerly, she recognized the pain in her head as a hangover. She'd never had much luck with beer.

"Why on earth did I drink it?"

Grit in her eyes confirmed a suspicion that she'd fallen to sleep crying. Then why did she feel like something wonderful had happened last night?

When she stood to walk to the minuscule attic bathroom, her legs balked. Good old country dancing.

She remembered driving home and later rebuffing Matt's advances, then running into the house. Nothing special occurred then.

So why did she keep feeling that something extraordinary had occurred?

Oh my God. Hank.

She dropped onto the bed. They'd kissed yesterday. Oh, how they'd kissed—magically. The kiss she'd shared with Matt later had been nothing in comparison. Poor guy had never stood a chance. It had all been about Hank since the day she'd landed on this ranch.

Hank had held her last night as she'd cried. She wasn't sure what to do with that memory— her first truly good one in a long time.

The bad memories had always loomed in her mind larger than the good, starting with her father's early death. If only she hadn't seen Dad die, hadn't watched the life leach out of him, his face pale and panicked, no peace in death, while he stared at her and tried to hold her hand. She'd been useless. She hadn't been able to save him.

How would it feel to drop the burden of those memories?

What had Mother said the other day? "Remember when your father used to send you to the store every night for Cracker Jack?"

Amy picked up the jade cat Dad had given her, rubbing her thumb over the smooth, cold stone.

Yes, she remembered the good times she'd

buried beneath the bad—how good it used to feel to have her father's love and his unwise but overwhelming generosity that used to make her and Mother laugh.

A memory teased her from the corner of her mind. If she could spin quickly enough she might grasp it. Then it was there, full-blown in her mind's eye—the childhood collection of every single prize she'd ever found in her boxes of Cracker Jack—treasured tidbits in an old cardboard cigarette box. Whatever happened to that collection?

She went to her dresser, grabbing anything she touched and putting it on—jeans and a pink sweater. She raced through brushing her teeth and washing her face. Then she ran downstairs to an empty house. How late had she slept? As she rounded the bottom of the stairs, she stopped suddenly. Hank walked toward her from the powder room at the end of the hall, adjusting his dirty white Stetson on his head. When he saw her, he stopped, hands slowly dropping to his sides.

Not a word passed between them, yet Amy knew that something had changed profoundly. Recalling her first day on the ranch, she'd watched Hank with a crowd of children swarming him, and thought he'd looked like an average man with not too much outside of a great body to offer a woman. But standing here now, desire radiating from him, she wondered why she'd so underestimated him.

She didn't know what to say. *Thank you for holding me while I cried for another man?* No, that wasn't true. She hadn't cried for Matt, or even for Tony, but for herself, for all of her losses and her own cowardice.

Hank was becoming a problem. A woman couldn't get involved with him and not fall for him deeply.

He tipped his hat toward her—doffed it like a gentleman of old—and brushed past her. That was Hank. A truly gentle man.

A couple of children ran up to him with one of the dog-eared books he read from every night—not a picture book, but what the kids called a chapter book. Hank lifted the kids into his arms and headed to a big armchair, where he settled them under an afghan.

He sat in another armchair and started to read.

Something was off. It took her a minute to register that Hank was turning the pages at an erratic pace that was at odds with what he said. Amy stared. It was as though he wasn't reading it, but rather making up the story as he went along. Strange. Why not read it the way it was written?

She watched him, his big hands holding the book, his too-long hair peeking out from beneath his hat. She pictured Hank turning back to catch her watching him, of a look in his eyes that she hadn't recognized last night, but did now in the light of a new day. Longing.

She blushed as the ghost of last night's embrace nudged her.

Hank Shelter—a man with perceptive eyes and welcoming arms. Oh Lord, she was in trouble. She'd fallen for him like a ton of bricks.

After wandering down the hall, she found Mother in her room, reading. Amy knelt in front of her like a penitent. Mother looked up, not surprised to see her there.

"Good morning, dear." She looked clear-eyed and peaceful.

"Mother," Amy said, "do you remember a collection I used to have? Of—"

"Of all of your prizes from your boxes of Cracker Jack," Mother finished for her, smiling, as if she'd been waiting years for the question.

Amy sat back on her heels. "How did you know I was asking about that?"

"It was the only collection you ever owned."

"What did I do with it?"

"You threw it away after your father died."

A pain started in Amy's throat and spread to her chest. She'd thrown it away. How careless and hard-hearted.

Mother's warm hand touched her cheek.

"After you stomped off to your room, I rescued the box from the garbage can, none the worse for wear after I cleaned off a little salad dressing and coffee grounds."

Thank you. "What did you do with it?"

"I stored it for you, hoping that someday you would want it."

Amy released a pent-up breath. "Do you think I could see it sometime?"

"Of course, dear."

Something had changed with Mother, too. She looked calm, unlike her usual querulous self.

Amy asked, "You like it here, don't you?"

"No, Amy, I don't like it here," she said, surprising her daughter. Then she grinned like an imp. "I *love* it here."

As Amy smiled and rose in search of breakfast, Mother stopped her. "I also love the dear man who runs this ranch. If you decide you don't want him, I'll take him."

"Mother." Amy gasped. "I'm not looking for a man."

She escaped before her mother could find the flaws in that claim. But a sudden revelation gave her pause.

In the years following Dad's death, she'd *needed* Mother to depend on her so that she could avoid her own emotions. Amy had feared they would overwhelm her if she ever let them out.

What if she'd had to face her own needs instead of tending to Mother's? Amy might have fallen apart. She recognized a part of herself that she'd buried for years—the emotion, and the need.

It was past time to be honest with herself.

As she stepped into the kitchen, a school bus honked in the driveway and she heard children running from all directions and out of the house.

"What's happening?" Amy asked Hannah, who bustled around the spotless kitchen, cleaning up after breakfast.

"Those kids are going home today," Hannah answered.

"Home? Today? But—" How could that be? Cheryl was leaving? Already? Where had the days gone? Amy's empty stomach flip-flopped.

"They are only here for three weeks," Hannah said. "You knew that."

"Yes, but I guess I lost track of time. I've been distracted by the accounting."

Hannah wrapped her arm around Amy's waist. "Come. We will say goodbye together."

It felt good to have Hannah's support when they stepped outside. The bus stood waiting for the children to board for their trip to Billings. From there, they'd continue on to their home cities.

Hank stood in front of ten boxes, with the children in a lineup beside him. He took a small white Stetson out of one of the boxes to place on the first child's head. Jenny snapped a photo of the child, who then threw her arms around Hank's neck and clung, whispering her goodbye in his ear.

"He gives one to every single child who comes to the ranch." Hannah pulled a handkerchief out of her sleeve. "Always has."

Cheryl ran to Amy and jumped into her outstretched arms. When she snuggled in, Amy was almost overcome. She clung to the child, afraid to let go, afraid she might shatter without Cheryl's arms to hold her together.

She'd fought it. Oh, how she'd fought the lure of this child's pain and love, but Amy had failed. She'd fallen for Cheryl after all, in a far-too-short week, and now had to pay the price with separation. She cursed the gods and fate and kismet that Cheryl wasn't hers.

Amy squatted on the grass and forced herself to set Cheryl away from her.

"Love you, Amy," Cheryl whispered, her eyes clear and dry.

"I love you, too." Amy's voice cracked. Cheryl's image swam through her tears. "I'm coming home to Billings soon and then I'll visit you. Okay?"

Cheryl's eyes held a touch of uncertainty. "For sure?"

"Wild horses couldn't keep me away."

"Not even Zeus?"

Amy's smile felt damp and weak at the mention of Hank's arrogant stallion. "Not even Zeus."

Cheryl grinned and ran back to the lineup.

She'd changed so much in the brief time Amy had known her, had grown from a timid child to one with confidence. How many miracles had Hank performed on this ranch over the years?

How did he do it—invite these children into his home, fall in love with them then let them go? Did his heart break every time?

At least Amy could see Cheryl again, but when would Hank ever get that chance?

The last of the children boarded. Amy cried when Cheryl put on her tiny white Stetson then climbed the stairs.

As Jenny started the engine and stepped lightly on the gas, a white cowboy hat waved in every window. Quiet and subdued, Hank watched the retreating vehicle. The ranch hands slowly drifted away.

Amy stayed behind under the willow, unable to leave, wanting to touch Hank, yet not knowing how to at this moment.

Hank continued to stand alone long after the bus had turned onto the highway and disappeared.

Mother walked past Amy and, without a word, took one of Hank's hands.

Amy joined them, taking Hank's other big hand in her own.

They stayed that way, keeping vigil with Hank in his grief, until there was nothing left in the air of the bright Sunday morning but the sound of a cicada calling for heat.

CHAPTER ELEVEN

ON MONDAY EVENING, Amy stared at the figures in front of her. She'd driven to Hungry Hollow earlier and picked up their books. They told a fair story of a ranch doing well with good management by a man Hank's father had hired years ago. As far as Amy could tell, he ran it competently.

Money came in from the sale of beef, but too much went out to support Hank bringing children here. A ranch the size of Sheltering Arms had enormous expenses, yet as far as she could tell, it all balanced. Just. No room for emergencies.

Still, what about that letter from the bank? Hank swore the bank had told him there was no problem. They hadn't sent a letter. She'd e-mailed Leila a few hours ago to ask more about it, but Leila hadn't replied yet.

Amy wandered to the kitchen and found Hank making a sandwich.

"Thought I saw the light on under your door," he said.

Amy wondered if he realized he'd just referred to the office as "hers."

A shimmering awareness passed between them in the quiet kitchen. It unsettled Amy and she rushed to change the subject.

"I've been going over the Hungry Hollow books. They look good."

He put a slice of bread on top of a mound of sandwich fixings, mashed it lightly with his palm, then picked it up. "Want one?" he asked.

She shook her head.

"Hank—" She started, then jumped as the front door slammed open.

"Hank?" a husky female voice called out from the hallway.

"Leila?" Amy looked at Hank. His expression mirrored her own shock.

"Yeah." He finished chewing the bite then set the sandwich on a plate. He wiped his mouth with a checked napkin and swallowed. "What's she doing here?"

Amy shrugged and called, "In the kitchen, Leila."

Leila strode in, her lanky six-foot frame almost vibrating with an air of urgency.

"Hank," she said, nodding, then turned to Amy. "I brought the letter with me." She handed it over.

How like Leila, Amy thought, to barge in with the barest of civilities, then get to the point.

Amy read the letter. The bank definitely said that Hank had not been making his mortgage payments. Amy knew that he had. *What* was going on?

Leila turned to Hank. "Well? Why haven't you been handling this? Is the ranch in so much trouble you can't pay the mortgage?"

Amy watched Hank grow still as he stared at the letter. His face took on a dark red hue. His hands curled into fists at his sides. Still, he didn't say a word.

And just like that, as if a light had suddenly been turned on in a cave, Amy saw it all: Hank's secret that he wouldn't share, his reluctance to help her with the accounts, audio books in his pickup truck, paying for everything with cash instead of writing checks. Reciting a children's story while flipping the pages out of pace.

Hank Shelter couldn't read.

She could scarcely believe that in this day and age a man Hank's age couldn't read.

She glanced at Leila. Leila obviously didn't know. How could she not? If Hank hadn't told her, how was he going to do so now, with his cheeks flaming with embarrassment?

"Leila," she said while watching Hank, "would you excuse us for a moment? Help yourself to a sandwich."

"Don't mind if I do. I drove straight here from the airport—except to stop and grab the letter. I'm starving." Leila picked up Hank's sandwich and took a large bite.

Amy held Hank's hand as she led him into the office and closed the door behind them.

Hank glanced at her face, then stared out the window.

"You figured it out, didn't you?" he asked, his voice low.

"You can't read," Amy said.

He hung his head and nodded, once, sharply.

"How did you make it through school?"

"The teachers helped me, let me take tests orally. Did as much as they could."

"But how did you graduate from high school?"

He shook his head again. "I didn't. They let me through as far as my football talents would take me, but said I couldn't graduate unless I got help."

"But what about your father? Why didn't he help?"

"It's dyslexia. The school didn't have the time or the funds or the personnel in a town this small to teach me one-on-one, and Dad wouldn't send me to a tutor. Said we had to keep it a secret that his son was too stupid to read."

Anger streamed through Amy like a flash flood. "Of all the ignorant things to say."

"Dad wasn't always kind."

"So I gather," she said. "You know what, Hank? I'm going to teach you to read."

He'd made it so far without knowing how to read. She marveled at how clever he'd had to be to not only survive but to also flourish, to realize his dream of bringing children to the ranch. He deserved a better deal than the one he'd been given by his lousy father.

"If it turns out I can't teach you," she said, "I'll find someone who will."

She rushed past him and into the kitchen. Leila had to be told so she wouldn't blame Hank for things out of his control.

Amy burst through the kitchen door and blurted, "Hank can't read."

She felt Hank behind her a split second before he yelled, "No!"

Leila turned an astonished face to Hank. "What? You can't read?"

Hank rounded on Amy and yelled, "Why did you tell Leila? It wasn't your secret to share."

"Hank," Amy said, "she needs to know."

"No, she doesn't. No one needs to know." He clenched and unclenched his fists at his sides.

"But it truly is nothing to be ashamed of," Amy said.

"Yeah?" Hank asked, and she'd never heard such scathing sarcasm from him before. "What about your secret? Let's tell everyone about that."

Amy recoiled. Now he was being cruel. *He's*

right, her conscience insisted. *You wouldn't want your shameful secret bandied about.*

Leila cleared her throat. "Why didn't Dad ever do anything about it?" Leila asked.

"You know how Dad was about secrets and family business."

"Yeah," Leila said, "I know *exactly* how he was." She slammed the napkin onto the counter. "Bastard."

Amy was glad she'd never met the rotten old man.

"I'll read the letter out loud." She sensed Hank's resistance. Nevertheless, she picked up the paper from the counter to read it, but the letterhead stopped her.

"Wait a minute," she said. "This isn't your bank."

"What?" Hank said.

"It's from a bank in Billings." Amy looked from Hank to Leila. "Why was your father dealing with a bank in Billings?"

"That's what I wanted to ask Hank." Leila turned to him.

He stared back at her, mouth open. "Me? This is the first I've heard of it. I haven't a clue what he was doing."

"Leila," Amy asked, "why didn't you tell me it was from a bank in Billings?"

"I thought Hank would know about it and tell you."

"Hank," Amy said, "it looks like they sent this to Leila because she owns the ranch. There must have been other letters before this one that came to the ranch, before they started talking foreclosure."

Hank spread his hands. "I got envelopes from another bank. Because I didn't recognize the bank's logo, I thought they wanted me to get a credit card with them or something. I threw them out. Banks send those things out all the time, don't they?"

Both Hank and Leila looked lost at sea.

"Guys, this is bad," Amy said. "This is a huge mortgage."

She glanced again between the two of them, but they continued to look bewildered.

"I don't have a clue what Dad was doing," Leila said. "I left all of that stuff to him. After he died, I thought Hank had picked up where Dad had left off."

"Wish I could have," Hank mumbled and Leila rubbed his arm.

"Okay," Amy said. "Here's the plan. In the morning, I'll go back onto your father's computer and see whether he was hiding anything."

She turned to leave the room, but said over her shoulder, "Both of you get some rest. I have a feeling the next few days will be busy."

"IT'S BAD, ISN'T IT?"

Hank stood in the doorway of the office

watching Amy, the mild belligerence in his stance warring with the steadiness in his gaze that begged her to be honest. He hadn't forgiven her since last night's blunder. She should have known that Hank wouldn't want her blabbing to most people, but his *sister?* Of course Leila needed to know. Underneath everything, Amy saw dread on his face, and a vague hope that the letter was indeed a terrible mistake.

She wished she could tell him it was. Instead she settled for the truth. "You are dangerously close to the edge. About six years ago, your father made some really bad investments and lost a lot of money, so he took out a mortgage to tide you over."

It had taken her awhile to find the info on the wily old coot's computer.

"The bank wants this mortgage settled immediately—paid in full by the end of next month. We can try to hang on to the land long enough for you to sell it. Once you settle what you owe on the mortgage, Leila will realize some profit."

When he didn't respond, only stared at her with a bleakness that unnerved her, she rushed on, "I *think* we can avoid bankruptcy."

He uncrossed his arms as his jaw dropped. "You mean we *might* go bankrupt?"

"I'll try my best to avoid that situation."

He shook his head. "What's our next step?"

"We sell the ranch. Fast." She said it quietly, but the awful news roared like thunder in the room.

Hank swayed. His skin turned a sickly gray.

And in this oddest of moments, she felt drawn to him. Her world dipped crazily.

She'd never had trouble separating the woman from the businessperson. Until now. She was emotionally involved—the very worst thing she could be for Hank.

"You'll have to lay off most of your ranch hands," she said, forcing herself back on track. "Hang on to a couple of them to keep the place looking good until you can sell it."

He rubbed his hands over his face, and her stomach turned over. How could she do this to Hank?

"Lay off the hands?" he croaked. "When?"

"As soon as possible. Tomorrow."

Hank sucked in a breath, then nodded.

"Tomorrow morning," he said, "I'll call them together for a meeting."

"Good."

He pinned her with a sharp look. "Will you be there?"

She hated these employee layoff meetings— full of disappointment, recriminations and, often, raging tempers born out of panic—but she would attend if Hank needed her.

After Hank left, Amy had a few minutes to

herself before Leila appeared. Amy told Leila what was happening.

"Okay," Leila said. "Do what you have to do. In the meantime, I'll go back to Billings to see whether I can gain a month or two's grace from the bank."

"Leila, you knew it was bad when you called me. I thought you were prepared for this."

"When I told Hank we'd reached the point of no return, I was trying to shock him into taking care of this. I didn't know things *really* were that far gone."

Leila shuffled out of the house. Her pace was so out of character that Amy nearly ran after her to tell her that she would fix the situation somehow, but that wouldn't be the truth.

She honestly didn't know what she could do for Leila and Hank to avoid the sale of their ranch.

THE LIVING ROOM echoed with the murmuring of the ranch hands. It died down when Amy entered the room and they turned curious gazes her way.

Where was Hank? Amy's stomach churned.

She felt him enter the room through the doorway behind her, a big warmth radiating against her back. He stepped to her side.

Everyone watched and waited.

Hank cleared his throat. "I have bad news. I can't—" He cleared his throat again. "I can't afford to pay you anymore."

As one, the people in the room stopped, their jaws dropped.

"What are you saying, Hank?" Jenny asked.

"I can't keep you on any longer." The pain on Hank's face burned through Amy. This was so much worse than dismissing staff in a large corporation, in which most of the employees were faceless numbers. These people were Hank's friends, as close to him as family.

Oh God, this was hard.

"I have to—" Hank tried to get the words out, then swallowed. "I have to—"

His shoulders slumped, he walked away.

For the umpteenth time on the ranch, Amy felt the weight of disapproving stares. People often confused the messenger with the bad news. That had always been part of her job, but it had never felt so hard.

"What the hell's going on here?" Jenny's voice was strident this time, angry and accusatory, as if Amy herself had brought this on them.

"Hank has to sell the ranch."

They broke into such a cacophony of raised voices that Amy had to clap her hands to call for silence.

"Unfortunately it's either that or bankruptcy," she said. "Hank won't be able to pay severance at this time. After the sale settles, we'll see what's left to divvy up."

Amy turned and left the room, to escape all of that shock and disappointment. She went in search of Hank and found him sitting in the backyard, staring at the fields he loved. He was about to be robbed of all this beauty.

"I don't understand how this could have happened in only one year," he said. "Dad never mentioned a word about money problems."

She squeezed his shoulders. What could she possibly say that he didn't already know?

HANK BLEW a long stream of air out of his lungs until they felt as empty as his heart. Funny that the sky was so clear, the sun so hot and life so normal when his world was falling apart.

A weight on his chest made breathing difficult. How many days did he have left here? Aw, hell. He rested his head against the back of the chair. He'd screwed up. If he were the crying type, his tears would never end. Instead all of his sorrow and regret balled up into a hard stone in his gut.

Staring at the clear sky, he whispered, "Dad, you crazy old man, you got your wish. I never let a soul see our private business. I never told anyone my problem. I never asked for help." Bitterness rose like acid into his throat. "And now I'm going to lose the ranch."

There was one person he needed to apologize to for his failure—his son. Despite everything Hank hadn't kept the ranch alive in Jamie's memory.

ONLY WILLIE, Matt and Jenny stayed on to clean and fix up the stables for the sale of the ranch.

Hannah cleaned the house from top to bottom.

Amy's mother took up knitting, smiling as she made mittens for the children she was certain would need them when they visited the ranch this winter. Amy shook her head. Mother was not senile, so why this refusal to face facts?

Amy consulted with real estate agents. It would take awhile to sell an operation the size of Sheltering Arms. She hoped they could hold on until then.

Hank moped. He wandered through the rooms and rode out of the yard with a dazed look on his face. He walked with sloped shoulders, a big man diminished overnight. Amy didn't know what to do for him, and her frustration grew.

She caught him one day sitting on the veranda, bowed forward with his hands hanging between his knees, and it started blood boiling through her veins.

This was so wrong. She had to do something.

She made an impulsive decision. "We're going to the bank in Ordinary," she said. She didn't want to build up Hank's expectations, but she couldn't tolerate seeing him do nothing.

"What?" Hank asked, his demeanor dull, listless.

"Stand up," Amy ordered, a drizzle of hope running through her veins—unrealistic, perhaps, but she was willing to try anything. "We're going to the bank in Ordinary. You've told me how special this town and the people who live around here are."

She grabbed his arm and hauled him out of the chair. "It's time to put Ordinary to the test. We're going to ask for help."

Amy got a whiff of Hank and waved a hand in front of her nose. "You need a shower." She looked him over critically. "Wash your hair. You need to look good for this."

Hank walked upstairs, his shoulders a little straighter.

Amy phoned Hank's bank and, five minutes later, she had set up an appointment with the bank's manager. She had two hours to spruce up Hank.

"Put on dress clothes," she yelled up the stairs once the shower turned off.

"What?" she heard Hank ask a split second before he appeared in the upper hallway wearing nothing but a towel wrapped around his waist above his long, long muscular legs. His chest hair glistened with moisture.

Amy swallowed. Hard. Oh Lordy, Lordy, Lordy. What a body.

She gulped. "We have an appointment with the bank in two hours." Her voice sounded squeaky, so she cleared her throat. "Put on your best dress clothes."

Amy ran upstairs to change, then went to gather any paperwork they might need.

When Hank came downstairs twenty minutes later, he wore a pair of black pants and a white shirt that molded to his biceps and pecs like a second skin, making his shoulders seem twice as broad as usual. His damp hair shone dark brown and whistle-clean against the snow of the pressed shirt. The tie he wore matched his pants—jet-black— with small white dots. His strong jaw was shaven clean of the dark stubble he'd been sporting lately. Amy had never seen him look so handsome.

Hank? Handsome? She nodded, tilting her head as if studying a piece of artwork. Yes, she mused. In his own way. It had to do with the strength of his personality and the depth of his caring—for the children, for his employees and for visitors to the ranch. She'd never known a man who possessed more compassion, and it shone out of him to meet everyone he dealt with. Yes, he was handsome in his own unique way. Handsome Hank.

Hanksome. Amy chuckled. Hank would like her made-up word, but he'd never accept it about himself.

"What's so funny?" he asked.

Amy shook her head. With his habit of self-deprecation, Hank would never understand.

"You need a haircut," she said. "You need to look your best today."

Hank swallowed and his Adam's apple bobbed in his throat. Nerves, Amy thought, about going to the bank with so much riding on it.

She stepped close to him and smelled the bracing citron of his aftershave. "Hank, we'll make it work out, one way or another. I'm striving so hard to make sure you don't lose everything."

"If I'm selling the ranch and no longer having kids up here, then I've already lost everything that matters."

Amy felt rotten. Yes, Hank was certainly going to lose everything that mattered.

"I have to tell you honestly, Amy," he said. "I hate talking to bankers, even if I did go to school with the manager."

"You did?" Amy asked. "Hmm, that just might help us."

"If you say so."

"You won't be there alone. I've done this dozens of times before, to work things out for clients. Trust me. I know what I'm doing. I know how to deal with these people. Okay?"

Hank nodded then gestured toward his head. "I don't know if Ralph can squeeze me in at the barbershop."

"I'm going to cut your hair," Amy said. Responding to Hank's raised eyebrows, she continued, "I used to cut Tony's hair all the time. He hated barbershops and salons."

Hank stilled. "Tony?"

Damn. She hadn't meant to let that slip. "My husband."

"Husband?" Hank looked at her as if she'd been lying since she got here, but why should she have mentioned Tony?

"My *ex*-husband. I no longer see him."

Hank raised one eyebrow in a silent question for more information.

"I'm still angry, raw. I can't talk about him."

"He was a rat, eh?"

She huffed out a laugh. "You could say that."

"What did he do?" Hank sounded sympathetic.

"He left me for another woman." That was only half the explanation. She would not tell Hank the entire reason Tony left.

"Do you want to talk about him?" Hank echoed the question she'd posed to him when he'd told her about his son.

She shook her head and Hank, thank goodness, let it go.

"I haven't been paying attention to my hair lately."

"Of course you haven't," Amy said as she walked away, expecting Hank to follow her. He did. "You've had your mind on more important things."

She led him to the back of the house, armed with her comb, her small nail scissors and a pair of sharp shears from Hannah.

"Grab a chair from the kitchen, Hank." She snagged a towel from the bathroom and stepped out to the patio. The shade on this side of the house cooled the air to a reasonable temperature.

"Should I bring a bowl, too?" he joked.

"Ha. Ha. I'll have you know I'm very good."

Hank set the chair near the edge of Hannah's garden, where the cinnamon scent of pinks permeated the air.

"I've always wanted a Mohawk." The twinkle in Hank's whiskey-colored eyes warmed Amy.

That's more like it, she thought, *let your natural good humor shine through.* If anything would help him get through today, that would.

"Take off your shirt," she ordered.

"Huh?"

"I said, take off your shirt."

"Why?"

"Because I don't want to get hair on it." What was wrong? Was he shy?

"Oh for heaven's sake, Hank, I've seen a man's chest before."

Hank's lips thinned as he tugged the tails out of his pants. Amy watched his trim hips swerve from side to side with his motion. Then he unbuttoned the shirt, one small white disc at a time, revealing his flat stomach and tanned chest one tempting glimpse at a time.

When he shrugged out of his shirt leaving his

massive chest bare, she knew she'd made a mistake. She was the one who felt shy now, standing in front of the most stunning display of male beauty she'd ever witnessed. How was she supposed to touch him now with the intimacy that a haircut required, and remain unmoved by it?

Gesturing for him to sit, she threw the towel around his shoulders to hide some of what tempted her, but it was like throwing a spoonful of water on a forest fire. Too little, too late.

Touching him gingerly, she positioned his head where she needed it, then pulled her comb through his thick waves, loving the chestnut highlights that ran through the brown. Combing the strip of caramel at his widow's peak that curled around her finger like a baby's fist, trusting and tenacious, she wondered how she was supposed to get through this.

She lifted a swatch of hair and clipped the ends with the scissors, lopping off a good inch. Circling his head, she trimmed the sides and back, lifting thick handfuls of hair then letting the sleek bunches slip through her fingers. The lemon of his shampoo lingered on the squeaky clean strands. Nothing sounded but the clip of the scissors and the chirp of a cricket on the still air.

She might have cut Tony's hair throughout their marriage, but nothing could have prepared her for the sensual experience it became with Hank. The warmth of his body smoldered in the distance between his back and her chest, shimmering between them like heat waves on asphalt. Her nails scraped the back of his neck and he shivered. A narrow band of lighter skin appeared as she trimmed, accenting how brown his skin tanned while he worked on the range.

The time came for Amy to cut the front of his hair and she stepped around Hank. Trying not to touch his knees with her own, she leaned forward to trim his hair, but found the position too awkward.

She cleared her throat. "Could you open your legs?"

Hank's gaze flew to her own.

"Please?" she said. "I need to move in a little closer."

"Yeah, sure," he said, his voice as rough as tree bark. When he spread his feet apart, she stepped between his thighs, then wondered if she'd lost her mind. As she leaned forward this time, she felt the moisture of his breath skitter into the V of her blouse, bathing her neck and upper chest.

Concentrating on the job at hand, she lifted a few strands of hair and snipped, brushing away the bits that clung to his forehead. Her fingers glided over skin as smooth as stones in the bottom of a shallow stream. Her hand shook when she lifted the next strand.

Tilting his head forward until it nearly touched the swell of her breasts, she worked her way toward the hair that she'd already cut on the back of his head. One of Hank's warm, hard thighs pressed against her leg.

She snipped the last strand, then froze, knowing she should step away but not wanting to. Running her fingers through the silk of his hair, she caressed his scalp just for the pure pleasure of it. Lifting his head, she traced his cheek and softly touched his lower lip, giving in to the joy of connecting with this big, tender man. Everything about him was huge and generous, like his heart.

Hank's other leg fell against her until she was cradled. The tips of his fingers nudged the front of her thighs, sending electric impulses shooting through her. A bead of sweat trickled down the center of her chest. Her blood meandered through her veins in a languid trickle.

Hank's head fell forward, nestled into the crevice between her breasts. His breathing accelerated, and she felt the humidity of it through her blouse.

She wanted to open her blouse and bra, to expose to Hank's mouth the beautiful flesh that men had adored in the past. To have Hank place his full lips around one of her nipples and suck. To feel his broad palms caress a pair of whole breasts. She held his head against her with a hand at the back of his neck, keeping still so she wouldn't destroy this precious moment.

She needed to cry with the pain of losing this opportunity. Why was life so damn unfair? She willed the tears pooling in her eyes to stay where they were. She'd shed enough already.

Hank lifted his head to look at her with all of his desire blazing in his eyes.

"Your hair's done. We just need to trim that mustache." She had to pretend that nothing had happened.

Picking up her nail scissors, she held his chin with one hand while she clipped.

When she finished, she straightened to find his intense gaze on her face, his intention clear. Moving slowly, he lifted his hands to her hips. He wrapped his palms high around her waist, his long thumbs caressing the ribs below her breasts. She felt the quickening of sexual desire and welcomed it. It had been so long. So damn long.

"Incomparable," Hank whispered, his voice raw with pain and wonder, and she knew he held himself in check.

She tucked her fingers into his hair and caressed the smooth skin of his temple with her thumb. "Beautiful," she whispered. Her knees shook.

As Hank ran his hands up her ribs until he covered her breasts, she dropped her head back and sucked in a deep breath, filling his palms with her full breasts.

On one breast, her nipple peaked, flooding her with intense desire and longing that echoed in a pull in her lower belly. She moaned and covered his hand with her own. On the other side, she felt no response. Nothing. Nothing but a prosthesis pressing against empty, dead tissue. Her scar. She grasped his wrist and shoved away from him, unsteady on her feet, her head pounding with desire and frustration and pure rage.

She wanted to tell him everything, but her overwhelming sense of shame held her back. "I—" She closed her eyes and hung her head. "I can't," she said raggedly.

Life was unfair. She had to live with that.

Letting her scissors slip from her fingers to the ground, she walked away, devastated by loss.

HE COULDN'T TAKE THIS ride much longer without going around the bend. She wouldn't give in to him, wouldn't give in to the attraction blazing between them. What the devil held her back? Had her bastard of a husband ruined her for other men? He wanted to tell her that he'd never be unfaithful if she was with him. That he'd never even look at another woman.

Some niggling uneasiness, though, told him that he still didn't have the whole story.

What the hell was happening here?

He rubbed his hands over his face. The frustration of it all was killing him, on top of losing everything else.

Forget about her, he thought, buttoning his shirt with shaking fingers. *Think of Amy as only an accountant. Forget about her as a woman.*

Right, and pigs could fly.

CHAPTER TWELVE

THEY DROVE INTO TOWN in Hank's pickup. Ordinary bustled on this midweek business day. Amy waved to C.J. Wright through the window of his candy store. She had found out that Mike Wright, who owned the grocery store across the street, was his uncle. Walter Wright, the minister, was his father.

She would soon be gone, and this sweet place that had coiled tendrils of affection around her heart would become nothing more than a memory. She sighed, wondering what it would be like to live here. That thought stopped her. Not go back to the city, to her home? She couldn't imagine giving up all of that.

Hank pulled the truck into a parking spot, then turned off the engine. He cracked the knuckles of his left hand. When he started on the right hand, Amy stopped him with a touch on his forearm. Hank froze and the muscles in his arm tensed until they felt like granite under her fingers.

"Take a deep breath," she said.

He did. His white shirt stretched across his chest.

Settling his clean white cowboy hat firmly onto his head, he stepped out of the truck. Taking her own advice and breathing deeply, Amy climbed out and locked the door behind her.

Hank opened the door of the bank for Amy to enter ahead of him.

The meeting went better than she'd hoped. On the strength of Hank's reputation in the community and his excellent record in dealing with the bank in the past, the manager had agreed to give Hank a mortgage large enough to cover the entire sum owing to the bank in Billings, on one condition. Amy had a week to come up with a comprehensive plan to make the ranch stop losing money. Otherwise, the deal was off.

It helped that Hank had gone to high school with the bank manager, had played football on the same team. There was something to be said for small communities.

Even so, those mortgage payments would be huge. How on earth would he pay them? Amy looked at Hank as they drove to the ranch, saw the tension on his face and in his shoulders, and had no idea how she was going to fix this for him.

LORD, how Hank had hated sitting in that office like a bump on a log, not understanding a thing that was happening around him and letting Amy take care of him and his business. He'd never felt so frustrated by his shortcomings. Aw hell, didn't that just go to show the differences between the two of them?

Realizing his hands ached from gripping the steering wheel too hard, he flexed his fingers.

How could he ever measure up?

He turned on the radio. Dwight Yoakam sang "A Thousand Miles From Nowhere" with his distinctive twang. Matt's favorite song. That thought led to memories of Amy dancing with Matt. Hank switched the radio off with an impatient flick of his wrist.

He felt her watching him.

"How much do the children pay to come to the ranch?" she asked. "I couldn't find that information anywhere."

"That's because they don't pay anything."

"Why not?"

"Those kids are inner-city kids living in poverty, or with parents drained by the stress of illness and big hospital bills. Some of their parents are unemployed or on welfare."

"Can you start charging the kids to come?"

Hank shook his head. "No. Emphatically no." *Emphatically.* Excellent word for how he felt. Dad had tried a lot of times over the years to get him to charge the kids. He hadn't done it then and he wouldn't do it now.

"But—"

"No."

"How about—"

"No. We don't charge those kids for coming and that's final."

Amy threw her hands into the air. It sounded like she mumbled "stubborn mule" under her breath. He would have smiled if the situation wasn't so damn serious.

"All right," she said, "how about if you start taking tourists on the off weeks? So the kids would come for three weeks, and then tourists for one or two and then kids for three. And so on."

Hank considered it, for all of thirty seconds. "That would give us no time for recovery. It takes a lot of work to prepare for those three-week visits with the kids."

"Yes, I can see that. I know everyone works hard. I guess the same goes for turning the ranch into a B and B?"

"Yeah. That's almost worse in a way, because you wouldn't know ahead of time when you were going to have company. Or how many."

He glanced at her briefly, watching her brow furrow. He could see that sharp brain of hers working. She brightened as if a lightbulb went on in there.

"How about if you turn the Sheltering Arms into a du—"

"Don't say it!" he shouted. "Don't even think it."

She cocked her head to one side and said, "How do you know what I was going to say?"

Hank pointed a finger in her direction. "You were going to use the *D* word, weren't you?"

"The *D* word? Do you mean *dude?* As in dude ranch?"

He ground his teeth, hating that word with a passion, one of the few words in the English language he really couldn't stand. That and coarse profanity.

"Hank, why does a dude ranch seem so much worse than a B and B?"

"Tourists who visit B and Bs are nice little old men and women who want to sit around in the country and be quiet. *Dudes* want to dress like cowboys, and walk like cowboys and talk like cowboys. But they aren't real."

He shook his head hard. "Uh-uh. No way. No dudes. Never. It'll never happen on my ranch."

He watched a slow smile warm Amy's face. "Why, Hank Shelter, you're a snob. Admit it."

"Yup," he said. "Damn right, I am."

"Well, well, well. The man has a fault, after all."

What she said rankled, but when he turned to confront Amy, he found her smiling broadly.

"I'm not a saint," he mumbled.

"No, of course not," she teased, then became serious. "How do you feel about approaching the government for charitable status?"

"I don't know anything about it."

"I don't, either, but I'll see what I can find out."

"Would that be enough to save the ranch?" he asked.

"I don't know," she answered quietly. "I don't think so, but it would help."

Hank wished he had a bunch of kids coming in today to take his mind off everything that was wrong with him and his ranch. He cracked the knuckles of his left hand. As he switched to do the same with his right, he noticed that Amy was frowning and staring out the window while she tore the tip from one of her perfectly manicured nails, leaving a ragged edge. He was pretty sure she didn't realize what she'd just done.

Man, oh man, if she was nervous, where the heck did that leave him?

FOR THE NEXT FEW DAYS, Amy worked like a madwoman. No accounting job had ever meant more to her than this one.

She researched getting charitable status for the ranch. Hank's father should have thought of it years ago. It could have saved them bundles at tax time. They did make a profit on the Hungry Hollow and used that to keep Sheltering Arms afloat. She suspected that could be a problem.

She found ways to cut costs and implemented them.

Cost cutting would help, but still, they needed

a steady income to pay off the mistakes Hank's father had made with his investments.

The letters started to arrive at the end of the week. Hundreds of letters addressed to her—from parents of children who'd stayed at the Sheltering Arms, from teenagers whose visits had been recent and from adults who had stayed here years ago as children.

The letters bombarded her with fifteen years' worth of love and respect for Hank.

Please don't stop Hank's work. Sheltering Arms is the most important ranch in Montana, one letter claimed.

I came to Hank with his first group of children fifteen years ago, a twenty-five-year-old man wrote. *I arrived angry and grieving. I left secure in the knowledge that I would survive whatever life chose to throw at me. Hank taught me that, and so much more.*

It contained a check for two hundred dollars.

He is a man beyond measure, another letter said. *A man who instills respect and pride and the will to survive in every one of "his" children. Yes, we are truly his children.*

Every letter spoke of unbridled love for Hank and the Sheltering Arms, and of the writers' own stories of success or salvation in spite of cancer, poverty and hardship—all starting at the ranch. Hank had changed their lives. It was that simple.

He had given them hope and self-respect and a belief in themselves.

Each letter contained money, some large amounts and some as small as one dollar, the latter most often from young children still living in the grip of inner-city poverty.

Tears gathered in her eyes after every letter.

The one that broke her heart, though, was Cheryl's. She'd dropped a quarter into the envelope. In large block letters, on a sheet of cheap foolscap, she'd written, *For Hank. I love him. You two Amy.*

Who had organized this campaign. Hannah? Willie? One of the hands who had already left? Whoever had done this was smart. Very, very smart. And fast.

These letters came just when they needed hope. And while the donations wouldn't sustain the operation, the funds would certainly help.

At dinner her gaze roamed the table, stopping at Willie, who wore a smug grin.

"You," she said, and knew before he answered that he had been the one to orchestrate those checks pouring in with the mail.

"Yep. Someone had to do something."

"That's a lot of letter writing and phone calls."

"Sure was." He applied himself to cutting the roast on his plate. "Took me an entire day. Was it worth it?"

She smiled. "Oh, yes. It was the perfect thing to do."

In testament to how low Hank felt these days, he showed not a shred of curiosity about their conversation.

"Hank," she yelled later. "Get in here."

He came running, his face panicked. "What's wrong? Are you okay?"

She pointed to the letters. "Look at these." She picked up a handful and read them aloud.

He shook his head slowly. "Can you beat that?" he asked, his voice wavering, his eyes bright.

Amy grinned. "I'll read the rest of them to you later, every last one. In the meantime, go hire the ranch hands back."

He stared at her. "You mean it?" he asked, his voice full of hope.

She smiled and nodded. "I still don't know how to get the children here, but get your ranch hands back to run the place."

Without thinking, she threw her tired arms around his neck, so damn happy that the immediate bad news was over, that she could give him back his ranch, for a while at least.

He tightened his arms across her back.

Surrounded by his hard masculine bulk, she ran her hands down his warm neck and across his hard shoulders, pressing her body against the fullness of his chest. As her palms flowed along his hard muscles, the nature of the caress changed, became an exploration. Feeling an acute ache inside of her to do more, she inhaled his essence—leather, soap, citrus and fresh air. His breath warmed her shoulder. Setting her palms against his chest, she pushed, moving away from him.

What if she gave in to temptation?

He ran his hands up her arms to her shoulders, barely skimming the sides of her breasts with his knuckles. She shivered and stepped away from Hank. Sadly. Reluctantly.

Putting on a professional demeanor, she said, "We'll work it all out somehow, Hank."

SHE'D BEEN IN that room for days.

Hank paced the dim hallway in front of the closed office door. Amy was already in there at 6:00 a.m., just like she'd been every morning this week. He had no idea what time she'd gone to bed—or even if she had—because the door had been closed when he went to bed at one.

"She in there already?" Hannah's voice startled him and he spun around. She stood with her hands on her hips. "She isn't eating enough to keep a titmouse alive."

"Did she come out at all yesterday?" Hank asked.

"Oh, yeah, she came out all right. She gave me this."

He glanced at the sheet of paper Hannah held. "What does it say?"

"I gotta cut down on the meat I'm feeding the ranch hands." She tapped her foot on the floor. "Those boys and Jenny work hard. They need protein. And she wants me to feed everyone some kind of cheap, prepackaged stuff." The tapping on the floor quickened. "For Pete's sake, I never served nothing from a box in my whole life."

So things were still bad. Hank had rehired everyone, but Amy had told them to stop drinking beer after hours—or to buy it for themselves. The ranch could no longer provide it. It was one of the few perks when the kids weren't around. There'd been a lot of grumbling about that.

Hank hung his head and stared at the toes of his boots. He couldn't get angry like Hannah or the hands—he didn't have that luxury. He knew the only reason Amy was doing all of this was to save his bacon. She'd become Public Enemy Number One so he wouldn't have to.

Hannah spun around and stalked to the kitchen, letting the door swing shut behind her.

He'd better talk to Amy. There had to be another way. He knocked and waited. No answer. He knocked again. Nothing.

Opening the door, he peered around it. Amy's head lay on the pillow of her crossed arms on top of a mess of papers on the desk. Half of her braid had unraveled and settled across her shoulder.

Hank cleared his throat. Amy didn't stir. He approached the desk and bent forward to study her face. She was sound asleep. Out like a proverbial light.

"Proverbial," he whispered. He liked that word. He liked Amy, too.

She looked exhausted. Shallow creases bracketed her mouth, as though she was tense even in sleep. The delicate areas under her eyes seemed almost blue. Her usually creamy skin looked dry.

He touched her cheek and she murmured. Tucking a strand of hair behind her ear, he tried to smooth it as best he could. She was always perfectly turned out. She'd be embarrassed when she discovered he'd seen her like this.

Crouching beside the desk, he rested his chin on his crossed arms, close enough to feel her breath on his face. He wanted these few moments of pleasure before he woke her. He'd missed her the last few days.

Her body was twisted, only half under the desk. Peeking under, he noticed that one foot was in a slipper and the other, stretched out alongside him, was bare. Pink nail polish dotted her toenails. She had tiny feet. He picked up the bare one and it sat in the palm of his hand. Her skirt draped across her thigh, leaving a portion of it and her long calf bare. She had real pretty legs.

"Great gams," he whispered.

He liked her like this, disheveled, without her usual strict control.

She stirred and opened her eyes, stared at him with an unfocused gaze. He had a minute to drink in the clear green color before her eyes widened and she jumped up, sitting ramrod straight and shoving her fingers through her hair. Since half of it was still braided, she got her fingers caught.

"You look like hell," he said, softening the complaint with a grin.

Defensive, she said, "You would, too, if you'd fallen asleep at your desk." Realizing what she'd said, she yelped. "Asleep? What time is it?" She glanced around the room.

Hank stopped her with a hand on her wrist. "It's just after six in the morning." He favored her with a wry smile. "It's Saturday, in case you don't know."

"Saturday." She nodded. "Okay."

He could tell she was still trying to get her bearings.

"You need a break," he said.

"No. I need to find a way to get the children back on the ranch."

Hank swallowed around the warm feelings in his chest. He cleared his throat. "What have you come up with so far?"

She grimaced. "Nothing other than registering as a charitable organization and cost cutting. I think Hannah nearly sent me out of the kitchen with a boot to my backside when I gave her the new budget," she said, with a smile tinged with wryness.

She was laughing at herself. A good sign.

Then she buried her face in her hands. "Hank," she mumbled, "I don't know what to do to make this work, other than tell you to stop bringing the children here. Turn the Sheltering Arms into a full-time working ranch to bring in more money. That isn't an option, though, is it?"

The look she shot him when she lifted her head was filled with pure misery. If she didn't care a heck of a lot for him, she had come to care for his ranch and his work with the kids. Maybe that was as much as she could do. He would take whatever she was willing to give.

"No, it isn't." He dragged her up out of the chair, steadying her with a hand under her elbow.

"You're dead on your feet. You need sleep," he said.

"I can't. Numbers keep swimming in front of my eyes the second my head hits the pillow and then I end up down here again, working."

"Then come out with me today. There's a big rodeo on. Everyone goes."

"I can't," she wailed. "I need to come up with a plan."

"I know, but if you spend one more day in here, you'll make yourself sick. Come on."

She was taking a break today if he had to throw her over his shoulder like a caveman. No *ifs, ands* or *buts.* He pulled her out of the office with her hand tucked into his. "First, we need to get you fed."

Pushing her into the kitchen and onto a chair, he said to Hannah, "Amy needs food. I'm taking her to the rodeo today."

Hannah nodded as she stared at Amy with a gimlet eye. *Gimlet.* He liked that word. Not sure if he was using it right, though.

"Amy wants food? Then Amy will get food," Hannah said, with a hard edge to her tone.

What is she up to now? Hank wondered.

"I need to visit the ladies' room," Amy said. She shuffled out of the kitchen.

"I'll be back in a couple of minutes. I need to check on my equipment for today," Hank told Hannah. "Is there coffee on?"

"Give me ten minutes."

Hank nodded and left. Ten minutes later, he poked his head in through the kitchen door. Hannah stood in front of the stove, her back to Hank. No Amy.

"Where is she?" he asked.

"Still in the bathroom. Tell her breakfast is ready," Hannah answered without turning around.

Hank frowned. Had Amy fallen asleep on the toilet? He'd invaded the office but wasn't about to barge into the washroom. He knocked on the door. "Amy?"

"Hmm?" he heard from the other side of the door.

"You okay?"

"Uh-huh."

"Can you come out now? Hannah has breakfast ready."

The doorknob turned and, a second later, Amy emerged from the bathroom. She'd tried to fix her hair, obviously without a brush. He knew the ponytail she'd pulled it into was barely civilized by Amy's standards. Her eyelashes were spiked with moisture. She must have splashed her face.

"Come on." He led her to the kitchen.

Hannah had set the table with cutlery and a red-checked place mat. She turned around from the stove and carried a full plate to the table, setting it down in front of Amy with a heavy thud.

Amy stared at the orange contents of her plate. "This is breakfast? What is it?"

"Macaroni and cheese," Hannah said with a righteous sniff. "The processed kind."

Amy gaped at her. Hank held his breath, waiting for the clash between the two strong-willed women with the dread of an engineer who knows he can't stop a runaway train.

Amy threw her head back and laughed. She jumped out of her chair, wrapped her arms around Hannah and rocked them both while she continued to laugh.

"You win," she said as she sat back down. "It was a dumb idea. We'll come up with something else."

Hannah crossed her arms at her waist while she tried to hold back a smile. "And the men? Do they get their meat?"

Amy collapsed into her chair. "Let them eat meat. What the hell, they can have their beer, too. Those were only Band-Aid solutions anyway." She dug into her pasta with more gusto than Hank had ever seen in her.

"What will we do, instead?" Hank asked.

"I haven't got a bleepin' clue," Amy said. She looked at Hannah. "Do you have any ketchup?"

AMY SAT in the truck and willed her racing heart to slow. Apparently Hank was participating in the rodeo. She didn't know if she could watch. What if he got hurt?

Every citizen of Ordinary had turned out, as well as those from the surrounding towns. Ranches from miles around must all be empty today.

She recognized faces. Angus Kinsey. The cowboys she'd met that day at Hungry Hollow. C.J. Wright from the candy store. Bernice Whitlow from the beauty salon, on the arm of a tall older gentleman Amy had once seen come out of the police station wearing a sheriff's uniform. No uniform today. Just a happy citizen like everyone else in the crowd.

As Hank steered the pickup into Rockwood Park, he trailed a steady line of vehicles that looked like a modern-day wagon train.

Hank had invited Mother to attend the annual rodeo, as well. Amy's arm bumped Mother's as Hank navigated the uneven ground. He slipped into a spot as directed by a young woman wearing an orange vest.

"Hey, Hank," she called. "Did you enter this year?"

"Yeah."

"All right! I'll be rooting for you." She directed a station wagon to the spot beside them.

The good mood of the people around them was infectious. Amy's spirits rose. *What the heck,* she told herself. *Just enjoy today and forget about the ranch's problems for a few hours.*

As she assisted her mother out of the truck, Amy noticed that the older woman's cheeks were full of color. Her head swiveled to catch all the action around her.

Hank's golden-beige chaps flapped in the breeze. What was it about them that made him look so good? Worn leather across strong thighs? Or the way they made his pants fit snugly across his backside? Amy didn't care, simply enjoyed the view.

The cowboys and cowgirls came in all ages and sizes. A small girl of about eight, wearing chaps and tiny cowboy boots, climbed out of the station wagon. Dear God, she wasn't competing, was she?

"Hank," the girl squealed, "I'm in the rodeo today. Are you?"

Amy had an instant vision of her on a bull like the ones in the photographs on the office wall.

"Yep, Angela, I sure am," Hank replied as the girl threw herself against him and wrapped her arms around his leg.

"What event are you doing today, Hank?"

"A little bit of everything. What are you entered in?"

"Mutton busting," she said, then ran back to the car to lift out a pink knapsack.

"Hank," Amy whispered, "isn't she too young to be involved?"

Hank narrowed his eyes against the sun. "Naw. She'll ride a little sheep until she falls off. They've got plenty of wool to hang on to. She'll have fun and she won't get hurt. Honest."

Hank moved to Mother's other side and they joined the crush of people heading for the stadium.

The meaty scent of charbroiled hamburgers and hot dogs wafted by as they passed food stands with lineups ten deep.

"Hank!" A burly, white-bearded man clapped Hank on the back hard enough to echo, but Hank seemed to barely feel it. He grinned and returned the favor.

"Walt, how're you doing?"

"Fine. You going to introduce me to your lovely lady friends?"

"Sure," Hank said. "This is Amy Graves who's come to stay on the ranch for a few weeks, and her mother, Gladys."

Walt shook Amy's hand with a paw the texture of a pinecone.

Then he turned to Mother and removed his hat, revealing graying hair mashed flat against his skull. He took hold of her fingers between his. "Has anyone ever told you you look like this young lady's sister 'stead of her mother?"

Mother blushed to the roots of her hair and smiled sweetly. "No," she said in her gentle voice. "No one has ever mentioned that before."

"I've often said the world is a crazy place." He shook his head mournfully, then turned to Hank. "Did you enter the bull riding or the calf roping?"

"Both."

Walt looked at Amy and Mother with a twinkle in his eye. "I don't suppose Hank has told you he wins every year?"

"You do?" Amy asked.

"Rodeo is a hobby of mine. That's all." Amy

saw the shadow of a smile hover on his lips. How like Hank to be modest even as he was proud.

"Where will y'all be sitting?" Walt asked.

Hank told him.

"I'll drop by later, if that's all right with you?" The question was directed toward Mother. She nodded shyly, then watched him walk away until the crowd swallowed the last sign of him.

Amy had never known Mother to react to a man showing her such marked attention. Amy wasn't sure how to feel about that. She'd never seen her mother with a man other than Dad so many years ago.

Reaching the stands, Amy remained in the aisle as Hank seated Mother on a cushion he'd brought.

"Do you need anything before I leave, Gladys?" he asked. "Water? A sweater?"

"No, dear, I'm fine," Mother answered, squeezing his hand.

Amy waited for Hank to brush by her so she could slip in and sit beside Mother. He smiled and doffed his hat, the gesture so second nature to him Amy doubted he even knew that he did it.

The man was a wonder. He treated everyone and everything as a gift, each and every day, and thought of life as a rare treasure.

Someone bumped Amy's shoulder, then murmured an apology. It got her moving to join

Mother, where she sat heavily on the hard bench, still mesmerized by Hank.

"He's a good man, isn't he?" Mother asked.

Amy stared at the hand Mother placed on her own. She blinked and nodded. Mother seemed to be able to read her mind these days. How? Was Amy becoming transparent? Was everything written on her face?

"Yes, he is a good man," Amy murmured, thinking about what-might-have-beens. "The best."

One thing became clear to Amy as she watched the different disciplines of the rodeo and the men and women who competed in those activities: half of the riders were very good and the rest were exceptional. The skill required of these people left Amy sorry she had ever mocked the rodeo or thought it a sport for crazy people.

A couple of old cowboys showed pretty well for their ages, but the rest were almost all young.

Jenny won in barrel racing, a fearless sprite with guts galore.

The announcer let the crowd know that Matthew Long had finished his bull ride and had stayed on for his full eight seconds. He'd finished in the lead with a score of 85.

"In the chute now is hometown favorite, Hank Shelter, of the Sheltering Arms ranch, riding Circle K's Whirlwind," the announcer intoned. The crowd went wild, but Amy sat with her arms crossed and her jaw tight. The irony of the bull's name didn't escape her.

How could a man Hank's age hope to win against so much youth? Yet everyone they'd passed when walking in had intimated that he could, and she'd seen the trophies in the office at home.

Home...

Why had she called it that?

His home. Not hers.

"Look," Mother said, grabbing Amy's sleeve and tugging, the grin on her face barely dimmed by her large sun hat. "There he is."

Straight across the arena, in the gate, Hank sat atop an enormous bull waiting for the prod Amy knew the animals got to propel them into the arena. She had a good mind to contact the SPCA.

Hank furrowed his brow and flattened his mouth into a thin line of determination. Even at a distance, his utter concentration showed on his face.

The bell sounded. The gate flew open. The bull charged out. Hank held on to the rope with one gloved hand and let the other arm fly straight up in the air.

Amy adjusted her baseball cap so the visor would block the action. She couldn't watch.

The crowd gasped and Amy peeked from under the cap with only one eye. Whirlwind bucked his hind legs perpendicular to the ground. Amy covered her mouth. Oh God. Hank. Hank leaned on the animal's back as he strained to stay vertical. Muscles in his forearm strained and bulged as he gripped the rope.

Whirlwind, huge at two thousand pounds, arched his back, tossing Hank forward—a two-hundred-pound man thrown around like a piece of flotsam on a crashing wave, his face within a hairsbreadth of smashing into the bull's head. Amy squealed. Mother grabbed her hand and held on. They both stood as the crowd surged to its feet.

Hank's thigh muscles flexed. He seemed to read the animal's mind, anticipating every move.

"Stubborn man," Amy muttered, but she couldn't contain the swell of admiration she felt.

The buzzer sounded. The longest eight seconds of Amy's life over. Still Hank hung on, his face coming dangerously close to the bull's head again.

"Get off," Amy whispered.

Hank let go of the rope and jumped from the bull in one fluid motion. Thank God. He landed on his feet and ran to the side of the arena where she and Mother sat. He laughed, his exhilaration and triumph evident.

Mother leaned close and asked, "Isn't he wonderful?"

"Hank Shelter takes home the jackpot today, folks," the announcer yelled, "with a score of eight-eight point five."

The crowd went wild.

"Eight-eight point five is good?" Amy asked. "But it isn't that close to a hundred."

"Oh, Amy." Mother laughed. "No one gets a hundred. Hank's score is *excellent.*"

"How do you know?"

"Hank told me."

Amy sat heavily on the seat behind her. How did the man do it? How did he vanquish men ten and twelve years younger than himself?

"He'll win big-time cash today."

Amy looked at her mother. "Hank told you that, too?"

"Hank told me the bull riders make the biggest jackpots because it's the riskiest sport on the circuit."

Amy snorted. No fooling.

Then she noticed the crowd around her, still cheering for Hank, crazy about him, the excitement running through them a palpable thing. They hooted his name, turned it into a chant.

Hometown favorite, all right.

Members of the audience leaned over from the front row and crowded the stairs to reach Hank—to touch his shoulder or slap him on the back. Or to ask for autographs.

Autographs.

The man was a rural legend—worth his weight in gold to these rodeo attendees. Even if she didn't fully appreciate the sport, she had to admire Hank's tremendous skill and the popularity it sparked—

Amy stopped and backed up her thought process. Hank was worth his weight in gold. *Worth his weight in gold.* A smile spread across her face. Eureka. She was a genius. An honest-to-God genius. Could it work? Would it be enough to save the ranch for the children?

Hank's rodeo skills were bankable.

Sheltering Arms ranch was going to have its own rodeo—with Hank Shelter as the main attraction and with Amy Graves pulling the whole thing off and saving Hank's bacon. She rubbed her hands together, anticipating the thrill of success.

Then she frowned. No bull riding, though, not even for the big jackpots. Roping and riding cattle and horses, but absolutely no bull riding.

"No!" HANK EXPLODED. Lord, the man could be stubborn. "No way am I turning into a circus performer." He spun her around on the dance floor that evening to an old country ballad.

Amy hadn't counted on him balking. The idea was brilliant. All Hank had to do was star in his own rodeo once a year. People would come from miles around to support him. What was so wrong with that?

"Hank, I don't really care whether or not you want to be a star. You already are one. These people love you." She brushed her hand across his shoulder and smiled sweetly to convince him.

"*Coy.*" He shot her a quelling look. "I hate that word and it doesn't suit you to be that way."

Amy scowled. "Oh, all right. I'm just trying to get you to agree with the most reasonable, exciting idea I've had for saving the ranch." Hank whirled her around particularly fast. "That is the bottom line here. We have to do whatever we can to save the ranch. Right?"

Hank stopped dancing and refused to look at her.

She scooted around until her face was directly in front of his. "Right?"

He heaved an enormous sigh and his shoulders slumped. "Right."

"Hank," Amy said. "Please trust me. I will do the whole thing tastefully. I will not make a spectacle out of you. Okay?"

He studied her for a moment, the two occupying a private circle of silence in the middle of the crowded dance floor, until Hank smiled and said, "All right. Do you have any notion of how much work it is to put on a rodeo?" Hank grabbed her and whirled her again—straight into Matt Long.

"Can I cut in, Hank?" Matt asked.

Ever the gentleman, Hank agreed, completely missing Amy's silent plea to stay. She wasn't comfortable with Matt. She'd hurt his pride and he seemed to take it as a challenge to win her over.

Grabbing her hand, he wrapped his lean, hard arm behind her waist and danced her around the floor, with a sloppy grin on his face that she was fairly sure he thought was charming. He was usually more adept than he seemed tonight. She frowned when she smelled whiskey on his breath. Her heart sank into her stomach. She did not like drunk men. They had a habit of being demanding and unreasonable.

"You having a good time here tonight, darlin'?" Matt grinned again. Definitely sloppy. "I noticed you've only been dancing with Hank. D'you only like the winners?" His grin took on a hard edge and his face turned mean. "Hank's left the rest of us eating his dust. Again."

He stumbled, taking Amy with him. It was all she could do to keep them both on their feet. For a minute, she thought they were going down, but Matt found his balance and righted them both.

"I've been a winner lots of times. How come you don't look at me like you look at Hank?"

What had she ever seen in Matt?

"Because Hank has character," Amy said, "and backbone. He doesn't have to rely on good looks or boasting to prop up his self-esteem."

Matt stiffened and his look became mulish, belligerent.

"He has a good heart," she continued.

Matt dropped her hand and raised his. She flinched. He stopped moving, his expression stunned. "What'd you think I was gonna do?" he slurred. "Hit you?" He shoved his fingers through his hair.

"I might not be St. Hank, but I don't hurt women." He loomed over her, but she sensed the truth in his words.

"I don't know about Hank being a saint," she said, "but I do know that he is a good man."

The fight seemed to whoosh out of Matt like air from a punctured tire. "Yeah. I know. The problem with guys like Hank is they leave the rest of us with too much to live up to."

He stepped away from her, looked like he would say something else, then grabbed her face between his two hands. He kissed her—hard and fast—then pulled back.

Amy darted a glance around the room for Hank, hoping he hadn't seen, or if he had, that he would know the kissing was one-sided. To her relief, he was nowhere in sight.

She saw realization dawn in Matt's blue eyes. "You love the guy, don't you?"

She stared at him, wide-eyed as a doe caught in the headlights, and nodded.

Suddenly sober, Matt said, "Well, I guess I can't fight that, can I?" He walked away with his hands in his pockets, a lonely cowboy in a crowded room.

Amy noticed someone else who looked lonely—and miserable—across the room watching Matt leave the building. Jenny. She had it bad for the handsome cowboy. Amy hoped that someday she'd either get the guy or move on, because she sure wasn't happy as things stood.

Jenny caught Amy watching her, and Amy couldn't hide the compassion she felt for the girl. Jenny's face crumpled and she turned away, pushing through the washroom door behind her. Amy started to follow but realized she had nothing to say that Jenny would want to hear. In fact, Amy was probably the last person Jenny wanted to see.

Amy walked off the dance floor wanting to think of more positive things than unrequited love. Something like the rodeo. The idea of putting it on gave her a thrill she hadn't felt in a long time. She smiled. For the first time since she'd been diagnosed with cancer, she felt fired up by a challenge. She wanted to save this ranch for Hank, and by God, she would.

CHAPTER THIRTEEN

THERE WAS SO MUCH TO DO—sponsors to contact, events to organize, people to talk to and a million e-mails to answer. Amy had to get the ranch onto high-speed Internet so she wouldn't spend the bulk of her days just uploading and downloading e-mails. She researched satellite systems and how to pay for another monthly bill.

Hank stepped into the office on Sunday afternoon and said, "You look like hell."

"Thanks, Hank, I needed that little pep talk."

He grinned. "I know exactly what you need. A heck of a lot more than a few words to perk you up."

Amy glanced up from the paper she was reading. "What would that be?"

"Time outdoors."

"Are you nuts? I have too much to do." She tapped a pencil on the desk. "We're going to start fund-raising. If you don't have the stomach for it, I'll do it."

"Okay, but I think you need to get out for a

NO ORDINARY COWBOY
246

while," Hank said. "I won't take you far. Maybe we can drive to the Hungry Hollow."

The Hungry Hollow. Amy's brain started working overtime. "Leila owns both the ranches, right?"

"Yeah." Amy heard the familiar regret in his voice.

She got excited. "I have another idea that's going to help us save this ranch."

Amy jumped up out of her chair. "We're going to have Leila give the Sheltering Arms to you."

"What?" He looked as though he couldn't believe his ears.

She twirled in a circle, then gave her forehead a soft smack. "Why on earth didn't I think of this earlier?"

"Because you're spending too much time indoors?"

"If Leila gives the ranch to you, you can continue to run Hungry Hollow for her, but you won't claim any of their profit as you're doing now."

She made shooing motions with her hands. "I need to call Leila."

Hank took a step toward her. "First, you're going out for fresh air."

"Hank, I—"

He wasn't listening. He dragged her out of her chair, down the hall and out onto the veranda.

The sun highlighted the landscape, turning fields, trees, distant hills to gold.

"This is so beautiful." The quiet wonder in her voice echoed her feelings. Somehow, when she wasn't looking, she'd fallen in love with the ranch, the country, the town of Ordinary. The community.

She turned to tell Hank as much. Her breath caught in her throat at the look on his face. Reverence.

In relaxed reverie, his face settled into smoother planes. His looks had grown on her—had become so appealing, combined with his gorgeous personality and rock-solid character, that she'd fallen in love with him. She could no longer deny it. Amy Graves loved Hank Shelter with all her heart.

She shook her head. *None of that nonsense. You don't need a man in your life.* But she did. She needed Hank. The longing to take him into her arms overwhelmed her.

What would he say if she told him about her flaw? Grabbed hold of her courage and just flat-out told him? Would he turn away?

"What's wrong?" he asked. "Why do you look so sad all of a sudden?"

He stood in front of her like a sentinel, a big solid sphinx, protecting her from everyone and everything, leaning too close for comfort. He tempted her, even as she wanted to crawl away from telling him the truth about herself. She turned her head away so he wouldn't see how far without hope she had fallen. The best man she'd ever met would know her secret shame.

"Don't turn away, Amy," Hank pleaded. "Look at me."

She refused to, until she felt his rough palm on her chin.

"I didn't want you to know. I didn't want anyone to ever find out about it, least of all you."

"Find out about what?"

"Never mind," she said.

"What do you mean, least of all me?" Hank asked.

Hope lit his face, brightening the dark concern of a moment ago. Amy knew she had to quash that tender expectation, for Hank's own sake.

"Hank, I—" She hesitated. "I care about you. Deeply."

"And I care about you." He slid his hands onto her hips. Their warmth nearly undid her.

"We can't do this. We can't do anything."

"Why not?" He bent his knees, so he could look directly into her eyes. "I gotta tell you, Amy, I've fallen for you so hard I'll never be the same again."

Why was he making this so difficult for her? "There's something I need to tell you."

"What?"

She swallowed hard. "I was diagnosed with breast cancer two years ago."

"Uh-huh. I suspected something like that had happened. Sorry you had to go through that, Amy."

Didn't he get it? Women often lost a breast, or a portion of it, when they had breast cancer. Hank knew enough about cancer to know that. Couldn't he connect the dots?

She got into his face, so there would be no mistaking *exactly* what her problem was.

"I lost a breast," she enunciated clearly.

A slow smile spread across his face. "Is that all that's holding you back?"

"Didn't you hear what I said?" Impatience made her voice hard. "I have only one breast."

He sobered. "That's awful, Amy, and I feel bad that you had to go through that. But did you honestly think I would reject you if I knew the truth?"

"Yes," she cried, exasperated beyond bearing.

"I won't. I love you, Amy. I want us to be together."

His declaration of love should have sent her to the moon, but she barely registered it.

"Don't you get it?" she asked. "I have an ugly scar on my chest."

"I wouldn't turn away from you because of that."

Her skepticism must have shown because he continued, "Over the years, I've seen what cancer can do to people and what they can live through. Plenty of people don't just survive. They go on to lead productive, happy lives." He shrugged. "Sure, some of the kids are still messed up. But lots of people are messed up. I feel bad that they couldn't work their lives out, but I don't pity them."

He leaned toward her. "Is that why I've been getting mixed signals from you?"

"What do you mean?"

"Sometimes when you look at me—" He avoided her gaze.

"When I look at you…?"

"You look like you want to eat me or something."

Amy choked on a bitter laugh. He was right. That was exactly how she sometimes felt—like Hank was a banquet on the other side of a wall of windows that she shouldn't open because she couldn't afford the cost of the meal.

"Then you turn away from me," he said, "like the last thing you want to do is touch me. Hey, I'm not the best-looking guy around—"

"Stop right there. I love the way you look."

"Then I guess we're going to have to do something about what we feel for each other."

He kissed her. She held her breath, savored the warmth of his lips. *Oh, Hank.* She closed her eyes, leaned into him and, with a moan, opened her mouth.

He tasted better than anything she'd ever known—like potent masculinity and gentle understanding and battle-hardened compassion.

She pulled away and swallowed hard. She wanted him. Somehow, she needed to work up the courage to expose herself to Hank and hope that he didn't turn away in disgust.

She wanted him.

"Tonight?" he asked.

"Tonight," she whispered.

HANK STOOD OUTSIDE Amy's attic door and listened to the silence of the house. He was free to make love with Amy. Finally.

He smoothed the hair down on both sides of his head.

"Casanova," he whispered.

A faint shuffling on the other side of the door let him know she really was in her room. He wouldn't have been surprised to find that she'd bolted.

His knock jarred the silence. He opened the door and found her standing beside the window in the dark wearing something filmy and pale and pretty, lit from behind by the light of the moon. The fabric of her nightgown whispered a sigh on the mellow breeze from the open window. Her blond hair fell around her shoulders.

Oh, yeah. This was right. *Indubitably.* Great word. Hank smiled, suddenly more sure of what he was doing than he'd ever been of anything, calm and confident.

Pale moonlight outlined her figure. Amy's hips flared from a narrow waist, into long, perfect legs. Her face in shadows, he couldn't make out her expression. His gaze dropped. He couldn't see what the darkness hid behind her gown.

"Can I turn on the light?" he asked, desperate to see her.

"No," she whispered. "Please don't."

"All right." Stepping into the room, he closed the door behind him, making sure the latch caught. It sounded loud.

"Hank, are you sure about this?"

He approached her and wrapped his arms around her. "More sure than I am of my own name."

She clung to his shirt and shivered in the warm room. He knew she wasn't cold.

"Come here." He took her hand and led her to the bed.

"Lie down," he said gently.

She lay on her back with her hands crossed below her breasts. Hank laughed.

"What?"

"You look like a virgin sacrifice."

An exasperated laugh broke from her and she set her hands at her sides, but her movements lacked her usual grace.

"It will be all right, Amy."

She looked away.

When he tugged the tails of his shirt out of his pants, her gaze flew back to him. No woman had ever looked at him as Amy did, with bottomless hunger. He unbuttoned his shirt and tossed it onto the floor. Her eyes widened. He removed his socks and lay down beside her wearing only his jeans, willing himself to take it slowly.

Pulling her against him, he ran his fingers through her hair. It felt like cool water flowing across his hand. He kissed her deeply, urging her tight lips apart.

She trembled when he reached for the ribbons that held her nightgown closed above her breasts. When the fabric parted, she pressed herself hard against him so he couldn't see anything.

"This isn't going to work," he said.

He spotted a bottle of lotion on the bedside table, beside a small jade cat. "Let's try something different. Roll over."

She held the edges of her nightgown closed while she rolled onto her stomach.

"Put your hands at your sides."

Now that he couldn't possibly see her scar, she

let go of her nightgown and rested her hands beside her hips.

Hank opened the bottle. The scent of jasmine assailed his senses.

He tugged her nightgown down past her shoulders and poured a few drops into his hand then rubbed his palms together. By the time the lotion touched Amy's skin, it was warm.

With long, even strokes, he massaged her shoulders and upper back. He felt the moment she started to relax, when her body settled into the mattress and the tense muscles of her neck eased. In slow, circular motions, he soothed her, until she seemed to barely notice when he slid the nightgown to her waist.

She had a beautiful back, strong and lean but soft and full in all the right places. Using firm pressure, he massaged the rest of her resistance away.

The tension was his now. Touching Amy was a bittersweet bliss, her skin a torment. He wanted her this very minute.

His big hands spanned her narrow waist, then molded to the swell of her hips. His thumbs caressed the dimples above her cheeks. He remembered his first glimpse of her the day she came to the ranch. He remembered thinking of full, curvy things like his guitar and pears, but none of his imaginings prepared him for the reality of Amy Graves naked as he eased the nightgown from her hips and down her legs.

She lay before him in splendor. He caught his breath.

He remembered the word he whispered that first day. *Exquisite.* It barely did her justice. For a man who loved words, they failed him now.

Pouring more lotion onto his trembling hands, he rested them on the cheeks of her perfect behind, his thumbs falling naturally to the deep cleft. Smoothing his palms down, his thumbs dipped into the sensitive crease at the top of her thighs. She gasped, arched a little then settled with a sigh.

By the time Hank finished caressing her legs and feet, his erection strained against the zipper of his jeans. Painfully.

Starting at the back of her knees, he kissed and licked the length of her to her nape, while she writhed beneath him.

Turning her over, he found her watching him, some of the tension back. He leaned over and kissed her, pouring his love for her into her mouth. She relaxed, marginally. He knew she wouldn't completely until he'd seen all of her. He pulled back and looked at her chest, pale in the moonlight.

He'd expected to feel compassion for her, but the anger took him by surprise—at God or nature, he wasn't sure which. The scar across her chest ruined the symmetry of a perfect body. Her left breast, the most beautiful one he'd ever seen, firm and sloping along the top to a full, dark nipple, flared round above her slim ribs. She must have been breathtaking when she was whole.

He rested his hand on her belly. It quavered beneath his palm. Still nervous. He had to reassure her.

Bending from the waist, he rested his fists on either side of her and kissed her scar. Her quick inhalation forced her chest against him. Running her fingers into his hair, she held his head still. He kissed her again, then felt the dam of her resistance break and her emotions overflow. He held her while she cried, caressing her hair, kissing her temples, her cheeks, her chest. Suckling her perfect left breast.

Gasping, she arched her back off the bed.

It unleashed the woman in her. When she wrapped her arms around his waist, pulling all his weight onto her, she pressed against him, kissed his lips hungrily, asked for more.

It was all Hank could do to get himself out of his jeans and into a condom.

They came together as strong as any whirling force of nature, passionate and demanding. He'd wanted to be gentle with her their first time, but she wouldn't allow it. She wanted him as much as he craved her. Reveling in her demands, he met every one, pushing her higher and higher until she stiffened, then shook, before he exploded with his own loving release.

HANK SIGHED, long and deeply. They were together now.

Amy ran her hands over his body, humming low in her throat, undulating her hips sinuously against him.

"Hank. Oh, Hank."

They made love again, even better than the first time, taking it slowly. Hank savored every inch of Amy's strong, fit body with his hands and his lips, as she savored him. She tasted of smoky florals, woodsy mosses, green leaves. He tasted and tasted and tasted more, skimming his lips over every smooth plane, swirling his tongue into every nook and cranny. Amy flowed down and over and through him, easing his loneliness, filling his aching emptiness.

"AMY?" he murmured in the early dawn, studying the interesting shadows the dim light made across the hills and valleys of her body.

"Hmm?" she purred like a satisfied cat.

"I never did finish that massage. I still have to do the front."

He searched the tangled sheets for the bottle,

but she stopped him by wrapping her fingers around his wrist.

"Slow down, there, cowboy. I have one stipulation."

Hank raised one eyebrow. "Yeah?"

"You can only massage me, partner, if you use—" she drew out the tension while she ran one finger along his lips "—your mustache."

He went still with the sudden, fierce ache in his loins, then felt a grin creep across his face.

"Yes, ma'am," he said obediently before dipping his mustache to the underside of her upflung arm.

She writhed and giggled.

SHE KISSED HIM in the morning after he'd dressed to leave her room, as she stood naked and unashamed in the broad light of day. Her scar no longer mattered. She owed it all to the big, beautiful man in front of her.

"Hank," she said, "are the women of Ordinary crazy?"

"What do you mean?" he asked.

"How have you managed to remain free and available all these years?"

"Aww. You know I'm as homely as a stump."

"You are a beautiful man."

"Amy, don't say that. It isn't true."

Anger shot through her and she grabbed his

face between her hands. "Yes, it is true. A man is worth so much more than his face. It is the whole man, your character and your boundless love, that makes you beautiful."

He shrugged and looked unconvinced. "If you say so."

She wrapped her arms around him, pressing herself full length against him, his denim shirt and jeans abrading her sex-sensitized skin. They hadn't slept a wink all night, yet she wanted him back in her bed already. She felt his immediate response. Leaning her head back until her hair whispered over her shoulders the way Hank's hands had last night, she laughed.

"Do you have any idea how sexy it is for a fully clothed man to hold a naked woman?" he asked.

"Do you have any idea how sexy your voice is?" she retorted. "Like fingernails raking sensuously over my skin." She shivered and her nipple drew tight. "Don't you think you feel beautiful to me?"

"If I feel half as good to you as you do to me, beautiful doesn't begin to describe it." He frowned. "I don't have the right words."

She held his face between her hands and stared into his eyes. "You don't need words, Hank. Everything you do professes your love." Kissing him softly, sweetly, she said, "I love you."

He closed his eyes and rested his forehead on hers, breathing roughly. For a split second, she thought he might cry. The emotion suddenly felt overwhelming.

"Get out of here, cowboy, before we both end up back on that bed."

His laugh filled the sunlight-drenched room. Grabbing her to him, he bent her back over his arm. Growling, he nuzzled her neck and chest scar, as if she could feel anything there.

Then he set her on the bed, and left the room, calling, "Eeeee-haaaaw," as he ran down the stairs.

She fell back against her pillow, laughing. She was in love with an amazing man. Her missing breast had turned into a nonissue. All it had taken was a little Hank Shelter lovin'. All of that fear for nothing. She sighed. The day was going to be far too long. She could feel it already—the desire to get Hank back up here and repeat last night.

FOR A BLISSFUL two weeks, Amy floated on a cloud. By day, she organized a rodeo that would help to save the ranch. She was aiming for September or October. By night, she made love with Hank. All night, every night.

Hank had done the impossible. She felt like a woman again, free to love completely.

The only argument they'd had so far was when Hank refused to wear his chaps—and nothing else—to bed.

How could she be the same woman who'd been so depressed when she arrived at the ranch? So joyless? How could one man make such happiness possible? A superstition that had taken root in her personality the day her father died whispered that it couldn't last.

"Shut up," she whispered back, but she shivered.

Stepping out of the office, she bumped into Hank.

"Hi," he said. "I was just coming to see you."

She stole a kiss.

"You look tired," he said.

"That makes two of us," she replied, smiling because the making of that fatigue had been so much fun.

He reached toward her, laid his hand on her arm and said, "Amy, I—"

She never did find out what he had been about to say, because Hannah came out of the kitchen at that moment, holding the phone toward Hank, her expression grim. "It's for you," she said, then turned back into the kitchen, but not before Amy saw her pull a tissue out of her apron pocket and wipe her eyes.

Amy's gut clenched.

"Hello," Hank said into the receiver.

A moment later, when he whispered, "Cheryl," Amy swung toward him. A chill skittered up her spine, raising the hairs on her neck. She started to shake her head, because she didn't like how Hank sounded or the bleakness on his face.

He hung up the phone and reached for her, but she moved away from him.

"No."

"Amy—"

"No," she shouted. "Not Cheryl. She can't have cancer again."

"No. It's not cancer."

"If it isn't cancer, then what is it?" The hard ball of anger in her gut rose through her chest and up into her throat, spewing all over Hank. "What the hell is it, if it isn't cancer? Is she sick?"

"No," he said, still trying to touch her, stalking her one painful step at a time.

"Tell me what it is." But Amy already knew. There was only one thing that made a person like Hank look so bad. She retreated but found herself butting against the back door with nowhere to go, with no choice but to face the truth.

"What—" Her mouth was too dry. She swallowed hard. "What was it?"

"She was hit by a car." He reached for her again, and this time she let him wrap his arms around her.

"A car? She survived cancer to be hit by a car?"

She wouldn't cry—wouldn't allow herself to feel the pain—but she let the anger through loud and clear.

"Where was her mother?" She hit Hank on the

chest with the palm of her hand. "Why wasn't the woman taking care of her?" She hit him again. "Why was she allowed to have her? Why would Social Services let her have a child she was too stupid to keep off the road?" With every question, she pounded his chest until Hank grabbed her hands, circling her wrists with his long fingers in gentle bondage.

"Cry, Amy, if it will help."

"No," she screamed in his face. She couldn't give in. That would make it all too real. Then she would have to admit that Cheryl was gone and that she would never see her again. Oh God. Cheryl was dead.

No-o-o-o-o.

"Why do you bother to save these kids if you send them out into the world to get hurt and to die? What use is your bloody ranch?"

"Amy—"

She tried to run, but Hank grabbed her arm.

"No." She clawed at his fingers. "Let me go."

"We can face this together, Amy."

"No. I'm not strong like you."

"Yes, you are." The conviction in Hank's voice cut her to ribbons. Didn't he get it? She couldn't stand to love and lose another person.

"You have more courage than you give yourself credit for." He shook her gently. "You didn't cave in when your father died. You pulled up your boot straps, survived and supported Gladys and yourself while you went to school."

"I had to." She turned away from him. "I'm not strong like you, Hank. I'm not a saint. I can't do this."

"Amy—" His voice broke, and she knew she was hurting him but couldn't stop. She didn't give him a chance to finish, just turned and ran away from him and the bad news and the love that always turned to pain. Always.

CHAPTER FOURTEEN

"YOU NEED TO GO BACK, you know."

Rain beat against the windows as Amy studied the view of Billings from her condo's living room and ignored Leila's comment. It used to stir her pride—that she'd scraped herself up from poverty and had earned the best for herself—but now she wished for more trees, a great large veranda she could step out onto, brown fields baking in the sun and fewer buildings hemming her in. A huge weeping willow nearby with a cozy wicker chair tucked under its shade would be nice, too.

Sighing, she turned from the wall of windows to stare down Leila, who sat on the edge of the white sofa, her brow furrowed, her face a mobile mixture of exasperation and concern.

"No," Amy said. "I do not have to go back. You needed someone to look at the ranch's books. I did."

When Leila opened her mouth to interrupt, Amy raised her hand. "You wanted me to advise you regarding the sale of the property. My expert opinion is this—don't sell. The finances have been salvaged."

"But—"

"I'm still working on the rodeo. I can organize it all from here."

The traitorous voice of her conscience whispered, *But you never taught him to read.* She couldn't do that long distance. She never used to break promises.

"I'm not talking about the finances and you know it." Leila raised her voice so Amy wouldn't cut her off again. "I'm talking about Hank."

Amy marched to the kitchen.

"I don't want to talk about Hank."

Acid churned in her belly. She'd never known desolation like this existed. Losing Hank was worse than losing a couple of pounds of flesh had been. She clamped her jaw on the grief that dogged her every waking hour. And her nights.

To add insult to injury, she'd not only lost Cheryl and Hank, but also Mother.

When Amy had left the ranch two weeks ago— okay, when she'd run from the ranch—Mother had decided to stay with Hank to deepen their friendship. It felt like a defection.

With a hard clink, Amy set a glass on the counter that separated the kitchen and living room. Grabbing a bottle of club soda, she filled the glass and added a slice of lime and two ice cubes.

She gestured with the glass toward Leila, who shook her head impatiently.

"I know you don't want to talk about Hank," Leila said. "But I want to know what happened between the two of you that has left him so miserable."

"Nothing happened."

"So the whole problem was Cheryl's death?"

"Cheryl's death was awful." Amy leaned her elbows on the counter and rubbed the cold glass across her aching forehead.

"Yes, I'm sure it was," Leila said with compassion. Her shoes whispered on the plush carpet as she approached the counter.

"But you can't stop living because someone close to you dies," Leila continued. "Hank didn't."

How on earth had Hank survived the loss of his son, his precious flesh and blood, to a death that didn't make sense?

Club soda bubbled up into her throat and she swallowed quickly. "But—but—how can he keep bringing those children to the ranch?" She pressed her hands against her pounding chest.

"At first, I thought he was nuts to start the Sheltering Arms. In the years since, though, I've seen the good that he's done, and how good it's been for him."

"But how can he keep going when someone like Cheryl dies?"

Leila shrugged. "He's a glass half-full kind of guy. He figures his brief time with her is better than not having known her at all. And—" she grabbed Amy's hand and squeezed "—they give so much back to him."

"I know," Amy whispered, her senses numb. "I've seen it."

She sipped her cold drink. The acerbic soda and lime soaked her dry mouth. "He has more courage than I have, Leila. I can't go back there and face those children again."

"You have more courage than you give yourself credit for. You survived two years of pure hell with breast cancer and an almost immediate divorce." Leila picked up her purse from a table by the door. "You're lucky to be rid of the rat, by the way."

Leila belied the harshness of that remark with a grin.

"Your father died and you didn't give up on life, did you?" she continued.

"I had no choice."

"True, and now you do. And that is the problem. The choice you make these days is to avoid intimacy so you can never feel that much pain and loss again."

Amy stared at Leila. Was it that obvious to everyone?

"I sound like a shrink, don't I?" Opening her

purse, Leila pulled out an index card on which were neatly printed a name and address. She handed it to Amy.

Amy took it from her, but the second she recognized Cheryl's last name, she cried, "What is this?" and dropped the card.

"Hank asked if you could go talk to Cheryl's mother, tell her how much fun Cheryl had at the ranch, and how her last few weeks were very special for her."

Amy's vision blurred. "I can't. Please don't ask me."

"*I'm* not asking you. *Hank* is." Leila paused in letting herself out of the condo. "It's time to screw up your courage and really live."

"Wait!" Amy cried.

Leila turned back with her hand on the doorknob.

"When are you going to screw up your courage?" Amy asked.

Leila stilled. "To do what?"

"To finally deal head-on with the big issue on the ranch." Amy tilted her head. "For a take-charge kind of woman, you've been appallingly lax."

"About what?"

"About Hank."

The color bleached out of Leila's cheeks. "What about him?"

"When are you going to tell him you aren't his sister?"

Leila's purse thudded on the floor. "What are you talking about?"

"Your father left everything to you instead of splitting it with Hank because it will all eventually go to Hank anyway when you die, won't it? He's your son, isn't he?"

Leila fell into a chair. Heavily. "How did you know?"

"I just put a few things together. Why didn't you raise him as your own?"

She took so long to respond, Amy began to doubt Leila would. "I had a brief affair when I was a teenager. I was young and foolish, experimenting, and got caught. Thought I loved the guy." Leila retrieved her purse from the carpet and fished around inside it, coming up with a tissue. "When Dad found out I was pregnant, he hit the roof."

She stood and paced to the window. "You have to understand what my father was like. He ruled that house with an iron fist. He hated for anyone to know his business. I could either pretend that Hank was my stepmother's child, or I could live on the streets without a penny to my name and raise a newborn infant on my own."

She exhaled a bitter laugh. "Dad would have followed through on it. He was a stubborn bastard. I was young and terrified. I went along with him."

"He's been dead long enough," Amy said. "Hank deserves to know the truth."

Leila let out a ragged sigh as she crossed the room. "Maybe. I don't know. I've loved Hank more than any other human being from the second he was born. He's my pride and joy. I've held on to this secret for so long, I'm not sure I can let it go. What if he hates me for never telling him?"

"Do you honestly think that Hank could ever hate you?"

"It worries me, but I'll honestly consider telling him one day."

Amy smiled. "That's enough for now, Leila."

"Okay. And you think hard about going back to that man."

Amy barely heard Leila go. The card with Cheryl's mother's address on it lay on top of the counter, staring Amy down. How could Hank ask her to do this? Her conscience whispered what Amy already knew herself to be: coward, coward, coward.

Visiting Cheryl's mother would be the kind thing to do. But Amy wasn't feeling particularly kind. She didn't want to think about Cheryl let alone talk about her. Amy had been doing her best to avoid thinking about Cheryl and Hank. Damn Leila for coming here today and stirring it all up.

Amy glanced around her condo and felt her control crack. She knew now there were men in the world who could love her despite a missing breast. Hank had given her such a gift by loving all of her including her scars—both internal and external. She couldn't go on living like this, alone for the rest of her life because she was too frightened to behave like a whole human being.

Smacking her hand on the counter, she decided the least she could do for Cheryl—out of respect for a perfect young child's memory—was to ease her mother's sorrow. Amy Graves was about to suck it up and do the right thing.

STANDING IN FRONT of the cracked, peeling door of an apartment in a building that smelled of urine and mold, Amy pressed a hand against her stomach to still the churning, then knocked.

The door opened, answered by a young woman dressed in a skimpy white tank top, black jeans and socks with holes in the toes. Amy had lost count of the piercings by the time the girl asked, "Yes? What do you want?"

Amy double-checked the number on the apartment door. She had the right place, but this girl was too young to be Cheryl's mother. She must be her older sister.

"Is your mother home?" Amy asked.

"My mother?" The girl frowned and touched one of the rings protruding from her left eyebrow. "She doesn't live here."

"Oh! I must have the wrong address. I'm looking for Cheryl's mother."

"That's me." The girl's lips thinned until her skin turned white around her mouth. "I mean, I was Cheryl's mama."

Amy stared at the girl and blurted, "You can't be serious." Then she clamped her mouth shut and noticed what she should have seen right away. In the girl's enormous, mascara-rimmed eyes was the premature wisdom Cheryl had possessed, forged by too much hardship too early in life.

"I'm so sorry," Amy said. "That was rude. It's just that you look so young."

"Yeah, everybody says that. Why did you want to see me?"

"I knew Cheryl when she stayed at the Sheltering Arms."

"You knew Cheryl?" The girl's beautiful dark eyes widened in her pale face. "Are you Amy?"

Amy couldn't hide her start of shock. "How do you know my name?"

"Cheryl talked about you all the time. I'm Janey. C'mon in."

Amy stepped into an apartment as neat as an officer's cot, stretched taut and spit-shined to threadbare perfection. The poor young woman owned so little. A small TV buzzed in the background across from a sofa shiny in spots and pilled in others. Secondhand, no doubt.

Janey walked to the TV and turned it off, all her actions slow and deliberate. "I keep it on for company." Standing in the middle of her stark living room, she looked like a lost sprite trying so hard to be grown-up. "Would you like a glass of water?"

She probably had nothing else to offer. Amy nodded. Janey stepped into the minuscule kitchen and took a plastic tumbler out of a cupboard. She ran the water in the faucet to get it cold. Amy couldn't remember the last time she'd had water from the tap.

She looked around her, at the base poverty of the place, and her heart sank. Cheryl had grown up in this, with no belongings, with none of the stimulation a young child would need to thrive and grow.

"Do you want to see Cheryl's pictures?" Janey asked when she handed Amy the tumbler.

"Yes."

"C'mon."

Amy sipped the water, then set the glass on a small table.

Janey led her to the only bedroom, a cramped, airless room, one small window looking onto the brick wall of another old apartment building six feet away. Two narrow beds lined the walls. Childish colorful drawings covered one wall, some of them little more than red and blue scribbles or bright yellow circles with big green circles for eyes and long, thin strips for bodies.

"Cheryl's?" she asked.

Janey nodded, obviously no less proud of Cheryl's work than she would be if she'd given birth to Picasso. She sat on one bed, so Amy took the other. On the wall at the head of Janey's bed hung a sheet of yellow construction paper with a big, red smiley face on it.

Amy remembered that Cheryl had drawn that one day on the ranch.

She sucked in her breath, trying hard not to dissolve into a puddle of grief on Janey's floor. She rubbed the ache in her chest. How often could a heart break with sorrow before it finally gave up and stopped working altogether?

The cheap night table between the two beds held a box of tissues and a picture of Cheryl. Amy picked it up with a trembling hand. Feeling her chin shake, she bit her bottom lip hard.

Looking at Janey through swimming eyes, she said, "She was so beautiful."

"Yeah. I thought so, too." Opening the drawer of the table, Janey withdrew a small, well-used cardboard box, with tape covering every seam. "Wanna see some photos of my girl?"

Amy took back every mean thing she'd ever said about the woman, every poor judgment she'd ever made about her competence as a mother. Cheryl had been loved without boundaries here in this modest apartment.

Janey opened the box with fingers whose nails

she'd bitten to the quick. Neatly arranged inside was a stack of photos. She handed the first one to Amy, a tiny shot of a newborn infant in a hospital cot. Not much bigger than a Savoy cabbage leaf, she lay swaddled in a pink blanket with eyes wide-open but unfocused, as if someone had startled her awake.

"She was small 'cause she was a little bit early, but all the nurses said she was real strong."

"Yes." Amy nodded. "I believe it."

The next shot showed an extremely young Janey lying in a hospital bed holding a slightly more alert Cheryl. Janey's eyes were rimmed with black pencil and her lashes coated with mascara, a young girl trying to look worldly and older than her too few years. By contrast, Cheryl looked pink and fresh, a tiny creature who hadn't existed a day or two before the photograph was taken. The awe in Amy filled her throat.

"Did you ever have a moment," she asked, "when you couldn't believe she was real?"

"Yeah." Janey took the photograph back from Amy and stared at it, smoothing her thumb across Cheryl's face. "Like I couldn't believe this little girl came out of my stomach the day before. It was weird, y'know? But really cool."

Amy looked around the room. There was no sense here of a man's presence. "Janey, do you see Cheryl's father very often?"

"I don't know who her father was."

"Oh," Amy said awkwardly. Anything else would sound judgmental or accusatory and she didn't want to do that to Janey. The circumstances of Cheryl's conception were none of Amy's business.

Janey stared out the window, the fingers clutching the photo on her lap turning white at the knuckles. "I was raped on my way home from school one night. I stayed late to watch a basketball game. It was dark out."

"Did they ever catch the guy who did it?"

Janey shook her head. "I never saw his face. He jumped me from behind."

Bastard.

Amy's hands clenched into fists. "How old—" She cleared her throat. "How old were you?"

"Fourteen."

Still a child. No wonder she looked so young in the picture. "Did you consider abortion?"

"My dad wouldn't let me. He said a baby shouldn't pay the price for someone else's sin."

"But he wasn't the one having the baby." Amy couldn't keep the sarcasm out of her voice.

"He was right." Janey's answering smile was calm and sweet. "I'm glad I had Cheryl. I'm glad I knew her. She was my precious baby."

She pulled a tissue from the box, blew her nose, then grabbed a fresh tissue to wipe the running mascara from under her eyes.

Amy leaned forward to take one of her hands in her own. "Why didn't you live with your father, if he wanted you to keep the baby?"

"There was no room for us with my sisters and dad, so I got on welfare and got this place. It was all ours," Janey said with a hint of pride. "My dad helped us out sometimes, but he just got laid off in the spring."

Amy stared at the back of Janey's hand, the skin stretched across her thin knuckles pale and blue-veined.

Picking up the photograph of Cheryl as a baby, Janey said, "I miss her all the time." Setting it back into the box and closing the lid with a snap, she said, "I want you to tell that man something for me."

"Which man?"

"The one who owns that ranch. Hank. You tell him from me that he is a good man. What he does with those kids is real great. The best thing ever." She shredded one of the tissues in her hand. "Is he your husband?"

"No. Why do you ask?"

"'Cause when she came back, everything Cheryl said started with Amy 'n' Hank. Amy 'n' Hank said this. Hank 'n' Amy did that." She sniffed. "Cheryl loved you both a lot."

Amy picked up a tissue and wiped her own face. "Does that bother you?" Amy blew her nose.

At Janey's puzzled frown, she added, "That Cheryl cared for us at the end of her life when she could have been spending more time with you?"

Janey's eyes widened. "Why would it bother me? It made Cheryl happy."

The quiet, unshakable absoluteness of Janey's statement knocked Amy for a loop. Of course. Those three weeks hadn't been about Janey, or Amy, or Hank. They were all about Cheryl, exactly as they should have been.

Amy stared at Cheryl's painted happy face, cheerful against the peeling bedroom wall. Yes, the little girl had known moments of happiness at the Sheltering Arms. Miracle worker that he was, Hank had coaxed smiles out of Cheryl by the time she'd left the ranch.

And, in that moment, Amy realized what she should have known from the start. Hank got the courage to bring these kids out to the ranch from his bottomless well of compassion. In spite of the pain he would feel when they left—or, heaven forbid, died—he wouldn't deprive the kids of a chance at happiness. Love wasn't about what you could get out of it, but what you put into it. And if you couldn't give in to that love for fear of losing that person, then you had no right to love him. And you didn't deserve love yourself.

In that precise moment, she knew she would stop wasting what time she and Hank might have on this earth. She was going back to him. Today. She was going to lavish him with all the love, honor and respect she felt for him, because he deserved it. He had earned more than the world could possibly pay him back.

And her fear? She would vanquish it. For Hank. Yes!

She would give her love to Hank for the sheer joy of giving. Consequences be damned. Her joy bubbled up like Moët & Chandon champagne in the finest Lalique.

She stood suddenly, surprising Janey.

"What will you do now that Cheryl is gone?" Amy asked, pacing five short steps to the door and back, a seed of an idea taking form, elating her. "With the rest of your life?"

Janey shrugged. "I don't know."

Amy turned to her with a huge grin. "Ever thought of living in the country?"

"I've never been to the country. But I want to see it. Yeah."

Amy took her hand and pulled her up from the bed, laughing. "Let's go. Pack your things. I'm taking you to stay at the ranch until you figure out your next step in life."

"You mean it? Really?" But Janey didn't wait for an answer. Pulling a knapsack out of the closet, she threw a few clothes into it, transformed before Amy's eyes into a chattering young woman barely out of her teens.

"Cheryl said the ranch was pretty. And that the horses were big. Oh, and Cheryl said the food was real good."

Amy couldn't wait for Hannah to put a little meat on Janey's bones.

Wait for me, Hank. I'm coming home.

ELATION FILLED AMY as she entered Ordinary, Montana—a town that, in her estimation, was anything but ordinary. Extraordinary was more like it.

She'd missed this warm community while she was in Billings, this group of people so interested in the common good that the odd few who were bad tempered or mean were only a blip on the pretty horizon under the Big Sky.

Amy knew she was back for good.

"Come on," she told Janey, who sat beside her in the passenger seat.

She got out of the car and breathed the fresh air. How could she have ever known how attached she'd become to this small town? How could she have known that she wouldn't miss the big city one bit?

Angus Kinsey drove by in a blue pickup. He waved. "Was wondering when you'd get back," he called. "Good to see you, Amy."

"You, too."

Bernice Whitlow swept the sidewalk in front of her beauty salon.

"Bernice! Hi!" Amy called.

"You're back. Good. How is your mother? She still needs to come in for those highlights."

"I'll make sure she does. How does tomorrow sound?"

"Ten o'clock?"

"We'll be here." Amy ran across the street to Sweet Talk.

The first time she'd landed in this town, she'd been scared and depressed. Today, joy oozed through her pores, along with the courage she would need to love her man for the rest of her life.

When she entered the shop, she turned megawatt smile on C.J. The smile he returned looked a little dazed. She knew she should tone down her actions but she was too, too happy and wanted to shout it out to the world.

"Hi," he said. "Whole town's been worried about you."

"No need to worry anymore. I'm here to stay."

"We all knew you'd come back."

"Yeah?" She replaced the dazzle in her smile with warmth. "It's good to be back."

C.J. noticed Janey. "Hi," he said, his tone gentle, as if he were talking to a deer he was afraid would startle and run.

Janey's face turned bright red, but she smiled and gave a small wave.

C.J. leaned on the porcelain counter. "What can I get for you?"

"I need twenty pounds of humbugs," Amy said.

"Twenty pounds?" he asked weakly.

"Yep. They're for my wedding."

C.J.'s head shot up. "Wedding?"

"Don't worry," Amy said. "You'll get an invitation. The whole town will."

"I'm real sorry, but I don't have that many humbugs at the moment."

"That's okay, as long as you can have them ready for my wedding day. I'll let you know when."

He wrapped the humbugs he had in the display case.

Amy stepped out of the store, her bag of candy heavy in her hand. "See you later."

A cow ambled down the middle of the road and Amy chuckled.

Oh, yes, the whole town would see her later, forever and ever, amen. She was staying here for good, if she could convince her big cowboy to take her back. She sobered a little at that thought.

"That was a cow," Janey said. "Walking through town."

"Yep. That was a cow, all right, in beautiful downtown Ordinary."

She put the car into gear, and drove down Main Street with the air conditioner off and the windows wide-open, so she could experience Montana country air to the fullest.

A cop in a neatly pressed uniform stepped out of the police station.

She stuck her arm out the window, waved and shouted, "Woohoooooooo!"

In her rearview mirror, his reflected image put his hands on his hips, shook his head and smiled.

She shot out of town toward her destiny.

CHAPTER FIFTEEN

"IT'S SO PRETTY," Janey said from the passenger seat.

The ranch house stood steady and serene behind the weeping willow that had welcomed Amy here on her first day.

Why had she worked so much harder for this ranch than she ever had for any other business?

Because the ranch was unsinkable. Something this pure and good couldn't fail—against any odds. It wasn't a business. It was a human endeavor of the highest order.

She breathed deeply the scent of dry prairie grasses.

A fullness in her chest threatened to overwhelm her with happiness. To hell with what-ifs and maybes. She would survive whatever life threw at her in the future, but she would love life and the ranch and the children and Hank for every precious second given her.

Tossing her hair over her shoulder, she laughed with the pure joy of the moment, and of the many moments to come with Hank. Would he take her back? She would simply have to make him, she thought, nodding her head for emphasis.

"Are you ready for this?" Reaching for Janey's hand, she squeezed it.

Janey turned sparkling eyes her way, the irises magnified by unshed tears. "Yeah. I want to see where my little girl had so much fun." Her broad smile, with the crooked eyetooth on the left side so like her daughter's, split a face that had become more youthful and carefree the farther they'd driven from the city.

"Okay, let's go." Amy stepped out of the car and ran to the tree, brushing her fingers through the leaves clinging to the branches with a determination that matched Amy's own.

Among the earthy scents of nature, she smelled cinnamon and smiled. Hannah.

The front door slammed. Hannah flew across the veranda and down the steps leaving Mother to follow in her wake. In the next instant, Hannah had her arms around Amy in a bear hug that belied her tiny size. Amy savored every breath-squeezing, rib-crunching second of it.

"It's about time you got home, young lady." Hannah pulled back and rummaged through her apron pocket, coming up with a huge white cotton hankie she wiped across her eyes. "Now, you stay where you belong."

Amy beamed a smile at Hannah. *Home.* On the ranch. At last.

Then Mother's arms engulfed her and Amy squeezed her back, so very, very glad to return to this dear, dignified woman.

"Mom," she whispered through shaky tears. She hadn't called her that in nearly twenty years. *Mom.* "I love you." The weight of Amy's ancient grief and anger and crippling sense of responsibility fell from her shoulders, leaving her buoyant.

Mom shook in her arms. A hot, damp spot formed on Amy's shoulder and cooled as Mom drew back. "Welcome home, Amy, darling."

One more quick, fierce hug then Amy pulled away, impatient to get to the man she loved.

"Where's Hank?" She scanned the yard. Where was the man she needed more than food and water and air?

"He is out behind the stables, with Zeus," Hannah answered.

Amy twirled to run to him.

"Who is this?" Hannah asked. Janey stood beside the car, fragile and hesitant in her tight black T-shirt, short red plaid skirt, heavy black mascara and countless piercings, a soft smile like her sweet little daughter's lighting her face.

"Hannah and Gladys, meet Janey. Cheryl's mama." It was the best introduction she could manage at the moment as she sprinted past the car and across the yard. "Fatten her up!" she called behind her.

She heard Hannah and Mom laugh as she passed the corner of the stable. Rounding the rear of the building, she stopped suddenly.

Across a long, long field, Hank sat atop Zeus with his back to her, tall and strong in all his vital, muscular glory, with the faded denim of his shirt stretched taut across his broad back and shoulders and biceps. His trademark white Stetson hid the deep brown hair whose lushness Amy knew by heart.

After an eternity away, her blood pounded at the sight of him, beating a frantic rhythm as she absorbed every last detail of the man.

The fullness in her chest swelled with his beauty. How could she have ever thought it would be possible to control her love for this man?

How much joy could one heart hold? Boundless, eternal, soaring waves of it.

Zeus ambled away from her, at a sedate pace for the horse who loved the feel of the wind as it streamed through his mane—like his owner.

Studying them, Amy realized that both horse and master had bowed heads and that Zeus had a listless gait. *Oh, Hank, what have I done to you?*

She'd destroyed his boundless enthusiasm. She had to make it up to him.

Just as she opened her mouth to call to him, Hank lifted his head.

"Damn you!" he shouted to the prairie, his raw, sexy voice tainted by misery and pain. And anger. Amy flinched. She started toward him, needed to soothe him, to beg his forgiveness.

Hank leaned forward at that moment, spurring Zeus into a sudden run. Amy's breath caught in her throat. Their quiet stillness of a moment ago transformed into raw power and energy.

Zeus stumbled. As abruptly as the run had started, it ended with Hank flying from the horse's back in a somersault that seemed to last forever before he hit the ground.

Amy gasped.

Hank rolled. Stopped. Lay still.

Amy covered her mouth with both hands. Bile rose into her throat. Not Hank. No. He couldn't be hurt. Not her Hank.

No! Rage filled her. She refused to lose him. Not now. Not when she'd finally come to her senses, when she'd finally gained the courage to truly love.

She raced to him as fast as her legs would carry her, but he was so damn far away.

Move, Hank, her mind screamed.

Not a ripple fluttered the grass that surrounded him.

AW HELL, he was gonna hurt tomorrow. He hadn't had the wind knocked out of him like this in years. He could feel the bruises forming already. He tried to get his breath back. Hard to do down here in the grass. Damn stupid that he couldn't stay on Zeus through a little stumble like that. Just showed where his head was these days.

Only one excuse. Amy. He missed her so damn bad. When he wasn't furious with her, he ached till he felt black-and-blue in every cell of his body. *Misery loves company.* Hah! That was a lie. The crew couldn't stand to be near him these days. Not Willie or Hannah.

He lay on his stomach on the damp earth, breathing in the fecund scent of soil and dry grasses, and heard Zeus circle around to come back to him with an even gait. No damage there. Good.

He should roll over to let the sun soothe the lids of the eyes he knew were bloodshot from lack of sleep. His stomach grumbled, but he didn't care. Couldn't eat these days.

Maybe he should stay here forever. Just lie in the middle of this field until the hay grew over him and everyone forgot that Hank Shelter had ever existed.

How was a man supposed to know that he lived only half a life until someone came along who completed him, who made him feel whole? How was he supposed to survive when she left, taking half of him with her?

Aw hell, Amy. Why didn't you just take a gun and shoot me? You would have done less damage.

He heard her calling his name. She haunted him. He expected her in every room, at every turn, and died a little when she was never there.

"Hank!"

Amy, for the love of God, get out of my head.

Footsteps pounded toward him.

Get lost, whoever you are. Leave me to drown in my misery.

Someone landed behind him, jostling his arm and ending with a jab of their knee into his side. Cripes. Whoever it was shouldn't ever go into a healing profession.

"Hank. Oh, my Hank."

His eyes flew open. All he saw was grass.

Sweet Jesus. Amy. She was real. Here. Amy, Amy, Amy. His pulse leaped at the sound of her beautiful voice.

Not melodic now, though.

Frantic. Scared. Miserable. Well, so she should be. Some devil inside of him raised his figurative head in the middle of the shock of her presence. *Figurative.* Great word.

He closed his eyes so she wouldn't know he was awake. A fine anger simmered over his joy. He should give her a taste of her own medicine.

Make her as low-down, mean-spirited ornery as he'd been without her.

He lay still. Controlled his breathing. Hardened his heart. Tried to stay unmoved by her touch.

"Help!" she screamed. "Help!"

Jeez. No one was going to hear her all the way out here.

"Hank, wake up." She tapped the side of his face with her palm, a little too hard in her haste and fear. Definitely not skilled in the healing arts.

She leaned her smooth cheek against his, surrounding him with her tropical coconut scent. He breathed discreetly but wanted to gulp mouthfuls of it.

He needed to touch her, but clenched his hands around hunks of grass against the urge. She'd put him through hell. But, dear God, she smelled good.

Grabbing his arm, she rolled him over. Good thing he wasn't seriously hurt. She might have killed him by now.

She fumbled with his eyelids and he quickly rolled his eyeballs up.

"Please be okay." Urgency threaded through her plea.

She tilted his head back and pulled his chin down, then breathed into his mouth. He nearly lost it, barely refrained from pulling her into his arms and devouring her sweet mouth. He almost cried when she pulled away, leaving his lips cool and damp.

He felt her fingers tentative on his chest, seeking something. Then she pressed hard on his sternum with her fists. He barely held back a grunt. For Pete's sake, she was supposed to check his pulse to make sure he didn't have one before she assumed he needed CPR.

She pressed again.

Jesus, she was going to kill him. He had to give her points for trying, but she'd be breaking one of his ribs right now if he wasn't padded with muscle.

He felt something round on his chest and realized it was her head.

"I love you, you big, wonderful oaf."

His heart hammered in his chest. She loved him! But did she have the nerve to follow through on it?

Keep talking. I'm listening. He was having more and more trouble not grabbing her and kissing the daylights out of her.

"I came home to marry you."

His breath caught in his throat. Marriage? Amy, his? Finally?

"I want to live with you on the ranch forever."

Forever!

His heart took flight like a prairie falcon.

Her soft, warm, feminine body fell on top of him. She was his.

That was it. A man could only hold back for so long. He wrapped his arms around her and squeezed hard, almost overcome with the exquisite pleasure of holding the woman he loved. *Exquisite*. God, he loved that word! He was never letting her go again. Ever.

He heard her shrieks muffled against him. When he eased his grip, she popped up to stare at him with her vibrant green eyes.

"You're all right?" she whispered, her voice tentative. "You're all right," she screamed, running her hands over his arms and shoulders and chest and—yes!—lower.

"Where are you hurt?" she asked. He raised a finger to smooth the frown from her forehead.

"Nowhere."

"What?" Confusion replaced the frown. "But—" She touched his head. "You were lying so still."

"Sweetheart." He nuzzled her neck. "It would take a fall a hell of a lot worse than that puny one to damage a head as hard as mine."

She stiffened in his arms. "You weren't hurt? At all?"

"Maybe a little winded." He licked the sensitive skin behind her ear. He knew she liked that. She didn't shiver like before, though. She still felt stiff.

"You were only a little winded?"

He removed his lips from her neck and grinned up at her. "Yeah."

The punch caught him in the solar plexus. The breath whooshed out of him.

Damn, he never had been much good at reading women. Lack of practice, maybe. He'd better get good at it fast.

She tried to wriggle away from him.

"Oh, no, you don't," he growled. "I'm never letting go of you again."

"You weasel," she yelled. Her hand landed on the side of his head, leaving his ear ringing. "Do you know how much you scared me?"

"Ow!" Grabbing her arms, he rolled on top of her. God, he loved her. Every gorgeous, enraged inch of her.

"You infuriating, maddening ox." She wiggled a hand free and grabbed a handful of his hair.

"Ouch. Sweetheart, easy." He got hold of her wrist. With her one cheek bright red against the green of her eyes and the blond of her hair, she looked like the sweetest angel in the universe, but—cripes!—she had a good grip.

"Don't you 'sweetheart' me, you louse."

She pushed against his chest, catching him by surprise.

She rolled away from him. He made a lunge for her, but ended up with a fistful of her shirt. She stopped rolling when it ripped. On her stomach on the ground, looking back at him over her suddenly bare shoulder—her lips red and swollen, her green eyes intense she looked like an adolescent boy's wet dream, like Woman Incarnate with long legs parted, rounded bottom covered by tight denim and half of her beautiful back exposed. Her hair spilled across her upper back. She shrugged her pale bare shoulder. Her lacy pink bra strap fell down her arm.

With that simple, careless, sexy as hell movement, she tempted him. He lunged for her. They lost control and were on each other, kissing, licking, rolling, tearing at clothes, until they lay naked on the prairie floor, surrounded by nature. *This is right,* Hank thought as he lay on top of Amy. *Here, like this, in this place.*

He looked around them, at the tall grass that masked them from the world, arching his neck to view the blue sky above that witnessed their lovemaking.

To whoever lives up there—God or Yahweh or Buddha or Supreme Being—thank you.

He lowered his gaze to the woman beneath him, watching him with her quiet, fine-grained intelligence. Precious. Unique. His.

"I love you," Amy said, with her heart shining in her eyes.

"I know," he said, suddenly serious. "I love you. I will marry you. Today."

He entered her slowly, steadily. She gripped him with her muscles, squeezing him with an exquisite sensation almost too beautiful to bear.

"Welcome home," they both whispered.

CHAPTER SIXTEEN

"WE WON'T GET MARRIED today." Amy lay in Hank's arms, sated and supremely, unreasonably, insanely happy. "We need to plan a wedding."

Hank groaned. It rumbled from his chest to resonate against hers. "Not a big one," he said. "I hate those things. Are you going to make me wear a tux and stand at the front of the church looking like a penguin?"

"I should, just to make you miserable," Amy answered. "You deserve it after the stunt you pulled on me."

"Which stunt? This one?" Hank asked, pressing his newly burgeoning erection against her belly.

"Not that." Amy chuckled. "You know what I mean. That was a cruel trick."

"I know." Hank sobered. "I was mad at you for running away."

She kissed his chest. "I'm sorry. It will never happen again."

Hank tucked her head under his chin.

She scratched her buttock. "This grass is itchy."

Hank's chest shook with laughter. "You got an itch that needs scratchin'? I'm your man, little lady."

She ran a finger over his lips, then pressed her palm against his stubbled cheek. "You need a shave."

He smiled and his eyes disappeared. She treasured his dear, honest face, with his strong jaw and bushy mustache, his mischievous eyes and perpetually lurking smile.

"Hank Shelter, you have been my salvation. I was so lost when I came here."

"Naw, you weren't really lost. Just a little confused."

"Well, I'm unconfused now and ready to take control of a few matters."

His expression became wary. "Like what?"

"Like inviting a few guests to our wedding."

"Do you really want a big wedding?"

"I want to invite our families and friends."

"That won't be so big, then."

"Yes, it will, Hank. I have a lot of friends."

"You're going to invite a bunch of your city pals?"

"Yes, most of these people will be from the city."

"They're not going to want to come out to watch me stand at the front of a country church."

Hank looked so miserable, Amy thought she'd

better be kind. "We won't have the wedding in a church. I'd like to have it here on the ranch."

He didn't answer for a minute. She could tell by his lowered eyelids and his mouth tightening into a line and his hands fisted against her back that a strong emotion gripped him. When he looked back at her with shining eyes and an enormous smile, she knew it was happiness.

"Let's go get started on that guest list," he said.

"Don't worry about the guest list. I'll handle it."

They got dressed, then started back to the ranch, holding hands and discussing money.

"Hank, you don't get it, do you?" Amy suspected this was what a good old-fashioned mosey felt like, wandering through tall grass in the evening while the sun set behind the trees.

Hank held the torn section of Amy's blouse closed with a hand on her shoulder.

Zeus trailed behind them, every so often nudging Hank's shoulder to rush him to the stables and the horse's dinner.

"I am very, very good at what I do," Amy continued. "Even beyond the accounting, I know stocks and bonds. I know how to mix investments so there's growth without exposing the principal to too much risk. I've done it for myself and my money is now yours. The ranch is safe."

Hank threw back his head and hooted. "Jamie," he yelled, smiling to the sky. "We're back in business." He looked at her seriously. "You're sure the ranch will be okay?"

"Yes. I will do everything in my power to protect it."

She stood on tiptoe. "And you," she whispered, kissing him. "Let's go plan a wedding, cowboy."

THROUGH THE WINDOW in her small attic bedroom, Amy watched for Hank to come riding across the fields that stretched clear to Hungry Hollow. She'd made him stay at the neighboring ranch for the past three days, swearing the entire community to secrecy on pain of death. She'd arranged a stupendous surprise for Hank. *Stupendous.* What a great word. She laughed. The man was rubbing off on her.

Elation. Another great word, and no better one to describe what she felt on her wedding day. Pure, unadulterated elation.

She strained to see into the distance. Still no sign of him. *Oh, Hank, it's time to come home.*

Sun beat onto the fields and a mild breeze ruffled the leaves on the trees.

Amy turned from the window when she saw a cloud of dust rise in the distance. He was coming!

The narrow, elegant skirt of her dress whispered around her knees as she scooted downstairs. Her heart beat hard enough to bounce out of her chest. What would he think of her surprise?

Pulling the front panels of her silk jacket together, she buttoned it before stepping outside.

Leila stood beside the minister under the weeping willow, waiting for Amy to join her. Janey stood on Leila's other side, every piercing filled with white pearls Amy had given her. Mom, Willie and Hannah sat in wicker chairs facing forward. Mom smiled when she saw her, Willie stuck a finger into the neck of his dress shirt to pull it away from his throat while pretending to gag, and Hannah grinned, sending a few rivers to crisscross with a few mountain ranges on the wrinkled map of her face.

The chairs behind them were filled with ranchers and ranch hands from the neighboring community and the townspeople of Ordinary.

When Amy looked beyond the chairs, her breath caught in her throat. She'd known her surprise for Hank would be good, but she'd had no idea just how emotional it would make her. Fanned out around the yard, across the driveway and into the fields stood hundreds of kids and young adults, each and every one wearing the white Stetson Hank had given them when they'd come to stay on the ranch—some as recently as this past summer, some as far back as fifteen years ago, when Hank had started this whole venture.

A young man in the front row smiled at Janey, the two silver studs in his bottom lip winking in the sun. Janey blushed and dipped her head with a shy smile.

Amy's elation rose in her chest. Love is in the air.

She rushed to the spot beside Leila in front of the minister, inhaling the essence of the ranch, satisfied to be home here where she belonged.

"He's coming," she called above the hubbub of the crowd.

The crowd cheered and clapped.

"Shh. Shh. He'll hear," Amy said. Everyone laughed.

"He's gonna know about it in a minute, anyway," Willie called out.

"You be quiet, Willie," Leila said.

Willie scowled but must have seen something on Leila's face to make his eyes widen.

Amy took a peek at Leila's face and was stunned by the heat she saw there. She turned back to Willie. He closed his mouth and sat back with a smug grin on his face.

She had so much good news to share with Hank in their future together.

Love is in the air.

She watched Hank ride around the corner of the house and draw Zeus to a halt, while the crowd turned to watch him. She knew the moment Hank realized exactly which "friends" Amy had invited to the wedding. His jaw dropped while he stared at the sea of white hats. One hand clenched into a fist, while the other rubbed his chest over his heart.

Her eyes misted over and she blinked furiously to clear them. She wanted to catch every nuance of emotion on Hank's face.

He pulled a white cotton handkerchief from his back pocket, took off his hat and wiped his forehead, swiping at his eyes as he went. Setting the hat back onto his head, he sat still with bowed head, the brim hiding his face.

When Hank lifted his head and met her gaze across the lawn full of guests, they were suddenly alone. With his eyes, he telegraphed the depth of his love for her, a love far deeper than any she'd ever known, and in that moment, she knew she was the luckiest woman on earth.

Someone clapped. Another person joined in, then another, and another, until the breeze on the Sheltering Arms ranch erupted with a thundering cacophony of love and respect for this man who had given these young people hope in their most desperate and vulnerable moments.

Hank dismounted and handed the reins to a ranch hand. As he walked the narrow gap left for him through the crowd to the lawn, he shook hands, touched arms, tapped shoulders, caressed young heads.

The only sounds now were the gentle murmurs

of Hank's "kids" as they greeted him, the most common refrain a heartfelt thank-you.

Amy wiped a tear from the corner of her eye.

One of Hank's former guests, now a virtuoso on the violin, started to play "Jesu, Joy of Man's Desiring." A hush settled over the crowd as the sweet, high strains floated on the gentle breeze.

Joy. Amy remembered her first day on this ranch, when she was sure she would never again in her life feel joy.

She knew the lyrics, hummed them to herself.

Hank started down the verdant aisle under the weeping willow to join her.

Yes, finally. Amy wanted to grab hold of life with both hands and trumpet to the world that she had fallen in love with a wonderful man who had, by his example, taught her courage. True courage. She hoped to continue the lesson for the rest of her life.

As Hank approached wearing his black dress pants, white shirt with black string tie and spotless white Stetson, she stared into his eyes— those dark brown, whiskey-highlighted mirrors of his beautiful soul that, at the moment, shimmered with more love than she thought one man could hold, and all of it hers. Then he took her into his arms and, before every living person who mattered to them, kissed the daylights out of her. All of him, hers. Every big, gorgeous inch of him.

He left her breathless, barely able to respond to the ceremony that followed or to the minister's questions.

"Wilt thou take this man—"

"Yes!" Yes, yes, yes!

Hank and Amy turned as one, partners for life, and the crowd whooped with screams of delight.

Almost every man, woman and child whom Hank had ever touched with his loving compassion threw their white Stetsons into the air, where they hovered and cavorted on the breeze like playful doves, set free by the love and sheltering arms of a remarkable man.

* * * * *

*Celebrate 60 years of pure
reading pleasure with Harlequin®!*

*Harlequin Presents® is proud to introduce
its gripping new miniseries,*
THE ROYAL HOUSE OF KAREDES.
*An exquisite coronation diamond, split as a
symbol of a warring royal family's feud, is
missing! But whoever reunites the diamond
halves will rule all....*

*Welcome to eight brand-new titles that unfold
to reveal the stories of kings and queens,
princes and princesses torn apart by pride
and power, but finally reunited by love.*

Step into the world of Karedes with
BILLIONAIRE PRINCE, PREGNANT MISTRESS
*Available July 2009
from Harlequin Presents®.*

ALEXANDROS KAREDES, snow dusting the shoulders of his leather jacket and glittering like jewels in his dark hair, stood at the door. Maria felt the blood drain from her head.

"Good evening, Ms. Santos."

His voice was as she remembered it. Deep. Husky. Perfect English, but with the faintest hint of a Greek accent. And cold, as cold as it had been that awful morning she would never forget, when he'd accused her of horrible things, called her terrible names....

"Aren't you going to ask me in?"

She fought for composure. Last time they'd faced each other, they'd been on his turf. Now they were on hers. She was in command here, and that meant everything.

"There's a sign on the door downstairs," she said, her tone every bit as frigid as his. "It says, 'No soliciting or vagrants.'"

His lips drew back in a wolfish grin. "Very amusing."

"What do you want, Prince Alexandros?"

A tight smile eased across his mouth and it killed her that even now, knowing he was a vicious, arrogant man, she couldn't help but notice what a handsome mouth it was. Chiseled. Generous. Beautiful, like the rest of him, which made him living proof that beauty could, indeed, be only skin deep.

"Such formality, Maria. You were hardly so proper the last time we were together."

She knew his choice of words was deliberate. She felt her face heat; she couldn't help that but she damned well didn't have to let him lure her into a verbal sparring match.

"I'll ask you once more, your highness. What do you want?"

"Ask me in and I'll tell you."

"I have no intention of asking you in. Tell me why you're here or don't. It's your choice, just as it will be my choice to shut the door in your face."

He laughed. It infuriated her but she could hardly blame him. He was tall—six two, six three—and though he stood with one shoulder leaning against the door frame, hands tucked casually into the pockets of the jacket, his pose was deceptive. He was strong, with the leanly muscled body of a well-trained athlete.

She remembered his body with painful clarity. The feel of him under her hands. The power of him moving over her. The taste of him on her tongue.

Suddenly, he straightened, his laughter gone. "I have not come this distance to stand in your doorway," he said coldly, "and I am not going to leave until I am ready to do so. I suggest you stand aside and stop behaving like a petulant child."

A petulant child? Was that what he thought? This man who had spent hours making love to her and had then accused her of—of trading her body for profit?

Except it had not been love, it had been sex. And the sooner she got rid of him, the better.

She let go of the doorknob and stepped aside. "You have five minutes."

He strolled past her, bringing cold air and the scent of the night with him. She swung toward him, arms folded. He reached past her, pushed the door closed, then folded his arms, too. She wanted to open the door again but she'd be damned if she was going to get into a who's-in-charge-here argument with him. She was in charge, and he would surely see a tussle over the ground rules as a sign of weakness.

Instead, she looked past him at the big clock above her work table.

"Ten seconds gone," she said briskly. "You're wasting time, your highness."

"What I have to say will take longer than five minutes."

"Then you'll just have to learn to economize. More than five minutes, I'll call the police."

Instantly, his hand was wrapped around her wrist. He tugged her toward him, his dark-chocolate eyes almost black with anger.

"You do that and I'll tell every tabloid shark I can contact about how Maria Santos tried to buy a five-hundred-thousand-dollar commission by seducing a prince." He smiled thinly. "They'll lap it up."

* * * * *

What will it take for this billionaire prince to realize he's falling in love with his mistress…?
Look for
BILLIONAIRE PRINCE, PREGNANT MISTRESS
by Sandra Marton
Available July 2009
from Harlequin Presents®.

Copyright © 2009 by Sandra Myles

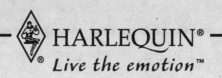

HARLEQUIN®
Live the emotion™

The series you love are now available in

LARGER PRINT!

The books are complete and unabridged—
printed in a larger type size to make it
easier on your eyes.

HARLEQUIN®

HARLEQUIN ROMANCE®
From the Heart, For the Heart

HARLEQUIN®

INTRIGUE®
Breathtaking Romantic Suspense

HARLEQUIN®
Presents~
Seduction and Passion Guaranteed!

Exciting, Emotional, Unexpected

Try LARGER PRINT today!
Visit: www.eHarlequin.com
Call: 1-800-873-8635

HLPDIR07

HARLEQUIN® *Romance*®

The rush of falling in love

Cosmopolitan
international settings

Believable, feel-good stories
about today's women

The compelling thrill
of romantic excitement

It could happen to you!

EXPERIENCE
HARLEQUIN ROMANCE!

Available wherever Harlequin books are sold.

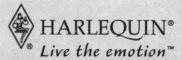

HARLEQUIN®
Live the emotion™

www.eHarlequin.com

HROMDIR09

HARLEQUIN®

American ★ Romance®

Invites *you* to experience
lively, heartwarming
all-American romances

Every month, we bring you four strong,
sexy men, and four women who know what
they want—and go all out to get it.

From small towns to big cities, experience
a sense of adventure, romance and family
spirit—the all-American way!

American ★ Romance®

Love, Home & Happiness

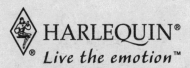HARLEQUIN®
Live the emotion™

www.eHarlequin.com   HARDIR08

HARLEQUIN®
INTRIGUE®
BREATHTAKING ROMANTIC SUSPENSE

Shared dangers and passions lead to electrifying romance and heart-stopping suspense!

Every month, you'll meet six new heroes who are guaranteed to make your spine tingle and your pulse pound. With them you'll enter into the exciting world of Harlequin Intrigue— where your life is on the line and so is your heart!

THAT'S INTRIGUE—
ROMANTIC SUSPENSE
AT ITS BEST!

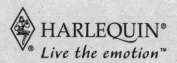

HARLEQUIN®
Live the emotion™

www.eHarlequin.com   INTDIR06

Harlequin® Historical
Historical Romantic Adventure!

*Imagine a time of chivalrous
knights and unconventional ladies,
roguish rakes and impetuous
heiresses, rugged cowboys
and spirited frontierswomen—
these rich and vivid tales will
capture your imagination!*

*Harlequin Historical . . .
they're too good to miss!*

www.eHarlequin.com   HHDIR06

SPECIAL EDITION™

Emotional, compelling stories that capture the intensity of living, loving and creating a family in today's world.

Desire

Modern, passionate reads that are powerful and provocative.

nocturne

Dramatic and sensual tales of paranormal romance.

Romantic SUSPENSE

Romances that are sparked by danger and fueled by passion.

Visit Silhouette Books at www.eHarlequin.com   SDIR07

Silhouette

SPECIAL EDITION™

Emotional, compelling stories that capture the intensity of living, loving and creating a family in today's world.

Special Edition features bestselling authors such as Susan Mallery, Sherryl Woods, Christine Rimmer, Joan Elliott Pickart— and many more!

For a romantic, complex and emotional read, choose Silhouette Special Edition.

Silhouette®

Visit Silhouette Books at www.eHarlequin.com

SSEGEN06

REQUEST YOUR FREE BOOKS!

2 FREE NOVELS PLUS 2 FREE GIFTS!

Passionate, Powerful, Provocative!

YES! Please send me 2 FREE Silhouette Desire® novels and my 2 FREE gifts (gifts are worth about $10). After receiving them, if I don't wish to receive any more books, I can return the shipping statement marked "cancel". If I don't cancel, I will receive 6 brand-new novels every month and be billed just $4.05 per book in the U.S. or $4.74 per book in Canada. That's a savings of almost 15% off the cover price! It's quite a bargain! Shipping and handling is just 50¢ per book.* I understand that accepting the 2 free books and gifts places me under no obligation to buy anything. I can always return a shipment and cancel at any time. Even if I never buy another book, the two free books and gifts are mine to keep forever.   225 SDN EYMS   326 SDN EYM4

Name	(PLEASE PRINT)

Address	Apt. #

City	State/Prov.	Zip/Postal Code

Signature (if under 18, a parent or guardian must sign)

Mail to the Silhouette Reader Service:
IN U.S.A.: P.O. Box 1867, Buffalo, NY 14240-1867
IN CANADA: P.O. Box 609, Fort Erie, Ontario L2A 5X3

Not valid to current subscribers of Silhouette Desire books.

Want to try two free books from another line?
Call 1-800-873-8635 or visit www.morefreebooks.com.

* Terms and prices subject to change without notice. Prices do not include applicable taxes. Sales tax applicable in N.Y. Canadian residents will be charged applicable provincial taxes and GST. Offer not valid in Quebec. This offer is limited to one order per household. All orders subject to approval. Credit or debit balances in a customer's account(s) may be offset by any other outstanding balance owed by or to the customer. Please allow 4 to 6 weeks for delivery. Offer available while quantities last.

Your Privacy: Silhouette Books is committed to protecting your privacy. Our Privacy Policy is available online at www.eHarlequin.com or upon request from the Reader Service. From time to time we make our lists of customers available to reputable third parties who may have a product or service of interest to you. If you would prefer we not share your name and address, please check here. ☐

SDES09R